CLOSE
BUT NO CIGAR

CLOSE
BUT NO CIGAR

HUMOR AND HOMICIDE WITH LP CINCH

JACK MANNION

A little murder, a little money,
a little sex, and a little funny.

iUniverse LLC
Bloomington

Close but No Cigar
Humor and Homicide with LP Cinch

iUniverse books may be ordered through booksellers or by contacting:

iUniverse LLC
1663 Liberty Drive
Bloomington, IN 47403
www.iuniverse.com
1-800-Authors (1-800-288-4677)

ISBN: 978-1-4917-0464-6 (sc)
ISBN: 978-1-4917-0466-0 (hc)
ISBN: 978-1-4917-0465-3 (ebk)

Library of Congress Control Number: 2013916856

Printed in the United States of America

iUniverse rev. date: 09/16/2013

CHAPTER 1

It was Monday morning, eight o'clock, and back to the grind. It was the start of another workweek, and LP Cinch was on his second cup of coffee, attempting to get his mind out of brain lock.

"Well, Cinch, did you do anything important over the weekend?" asked Irv Kluger, a fellow probation officer, who was seated at his work desk next to LP's.

LP sipped his coffee for a second and said, "Nothing much. Yesterday I took a bus up to Reno to check my luck and to visit my money, you might say. I at least saved the cost of gas."

"Did you win anything?"

"Well, of course not. My system on the roulette wheel never fails. I never win, but I don't lose a lot, and it takes those robbers a long time to get my forty or fifty bucks. I usually buy ten-cent chips and bet the minimum, one chip on four different numbers on each roll of the ball. Occasionally I hit a number, and it keeps me going for a while. When I lose it all, I hang around awhile and crank a few one-armed bandits and then grab the next bus back home. Someday I'll get hot and end up owning one of those

1

joints. End of joke, laugh here. What about you? What were you up to over the weekend?"

Irv said, "Me and a couple of guys drove over and watched the Giants win another game. They're in first place now and looking like they'll go all the way."

LP enjoyed ribbing Irv when he could, and Irv, being a Chicago transplant and a sports nut, would always get worked up when you brought up the subject of the Chicago Cubs or the Bears. LP decided to trip his button a bit and said, "That reminds me, Irv, your favorite Cubs are really stinking up things again this year. I think you ought to give up on those rubes. You know, if I'm not mistaken, the last time they were in a World Series was in 1946." LP thought for a second and continued, "By my calculations, that was around forty years ago."

Irv said with a growl, "Come on, Cinch, don't rub it in. Be patient. It will happen again."

"Yeah," said LP, "we know, we know. They'll always be close, but no cigar, though, old buddy."

Cinch glanced around the crowded room and observed that the half-dozen other probation officers were getting organized for their workday, and he decided he better do the same. He had a lot to do, as always. Today he would spend his time in the field running down probationers. But as he went through the necessary preparations, his mind kept wandering back to the statement he had made to Irv. He thought, *I'm as bad as or worse than the Cubs. That's me exactly.*

Today LP felt a little sorrier for himself than usual. He had been in this line of work for about half a lifetime, it seemed. In a business like this, for people with a little experience under their belts and extended time at the job, some sort of promotion or advancement should have been a possibility. But over the years, LP hadn't advanced past buck private. He had been bounced around, like a lot of other unfortunates, from one assignment to another. He'd been moved around, but the movement wasn't upward. He had been assigned to adult court, juvenile court, field supervision, and other jobs, but none were considered for advancement in responsibility, prestige, or financial gain. He was stuck at the bottom of the pile. Although his current assignment was the softest, least-stressful job he'd had so far, he was feeling burned out. He was always close but no cigar.

Unless you've been around for a while, the phrase "close but not cigar" is probably meaningless to you, but for an old-timer like LP, the term was very descriptive of his present state of mind. Years ago at carnivals and amusement parks, there was a particularly popular game of skill and strength. In the game, a man could show off his brute strength to his girlfriend or his pals. For fifty cents, all he had to do was ring a gong by slamming a sledgehammer down on a board hard enough to send a ball up a fifteen-foot pole and ring the gong at the top. If he succeeded, he received a cheap cigar and maybe a pat on the back. Failure meant he was seen as a bit of a wimp and a loser. Usually the carnies would shout after the loser's effort, "Close but no cigar. Try again (sucker)."

This morning LP didn't think he was a total loser, but perhaps he was a bit like the sucker. He had a lot of years on his job, and he still wasn't ringing the gong. He was still at the bottom rung of the stairway to wealth, fame, and stature.

As he dragged his mind through the pits of self-pity, he remembered a time in his youth when he was a teenager in a small Montana town. There was a sad but funny local man who worked on a ranch near the town. He seldom came into town, but periodically he would come and go on a bender. He'd drink in all of the local dives and stay drunk for days. One day on one of his benders, he was lying passed out on the sidewalk in front of one of his favorite beer joints. He woke up, remained sitting on the pavement, and began to look around. LP and several of his teenage pals were standing nearby.

The drunk looked around for several minutes and finally asked, "Can anybody tell me how long I've been in this condition?"

He got a real laugh out of all of them, but he had hit a bull's-eye on how LP was feeling on this Monday morning at work. "Can anybody tell me how long I've been in this condition?" LP felt he was making about as much progress in life as the old binge drinker.

LP recalled another occasion from when he lived in Omaha. He had a buddy who also had a problem of enjoying his booze too much. One Monday morning, LP asked his pal where he had been over the weekend. He hadn't seen him around for several days. His buddy said he was doing a little drinking on Friday after work, and one drink led to another. On Sunday morning, he woke up in a strange bed in a strange room. He said he realized he was in a hotel room but couldn't remember how he had gotten there. He called down to the hotel's front desk and asked the clerk the name of the hotel. The clerk gave him the name, but he didn't recognize the name, so he asked the clerk, "What street is the hotel on?" The clerk gave him the street address, and this also was unfamiliar. Finally, he asked the clerk, "Well, what town are we in?"

The clerk said, "Welcome to Lincoln, Nebraska, sir."

He said he hung up and asked himself, *What am I doing here? Boy, I must have had a great time. I'm about eighty miles from home, and I don't even own a car.*

LP thought to himself, *I'm almost in the same boat as those two drunks. Both of them were asking for answers. I'm as sober as a judge and asking the same questions as they were. Well, join the club. I'm beginning to think the answer to question number one—"How long have I been in this condition?"—is a definite "too long." And the answer to question number two—"What am I doing here?"—is a little harder to figure out, but it could easily be, "Darned if I know." But I do have a car if I decide on a quick getaway. There must be a remedy somewhere.*

But LP had to get his mind back to reality—to the real world. He had to admit to himself that his current assignment was much less stressful than previous assignments and was far more interesting. Supervising probationers meant a good percentage of his time was spent out of the office and running around the city. On the other hand, the office had all the appeal of living in the inside a discarded shoe. Cramped? Consider working in a small, windowless room with eight or nine other angry drones, each with a large work desk covered with piles of paperwork, a large file cabinet containing about 120 to 150 case files inside, phones ringing, voices banging off the block walls, bright, stark neon lights from above, and notes, reminders, and notices stuck to the walls next to each desk.

Being out in the field was different. That was where the people and the action were. At times it could be almost like a circus. You never knew what to expect. The unexpected was the norm. It was almost fun. The way some probationers acted and lived could really open your eyes. It was like a free education.

Yes, LP had to deal with the real world. It wasn't going to change for him. He considered all his fellow workers—fifty or sixty men and women in this branch office. They all seemed to be well adjusted to their jobs and full of ambition. They were in the same boat as he was, but they weren't dragging around like he was or feeling sorry for themselves. He had to admit to himself that he was a bit of a loner. He didn't hang out with any of them after work or socially, like many of the others did. When his day was finished, he was far removed from the scene. He got along well with most everyone, but yes, he had to admit he preferred to be alone. He was a little outspoken at times, perhaps, but was a sort of an invisible man and was aging. He was just another faceless piece of furniture who was dedicated to doing his job to the best of his abilities. He was also currently in a state of restlessness.

He remembered one past incident that might have put a bit of a jacket on him. Years earlier, when he had been transferred to juvenile court, he was unfortunate to find himself in a unit that had an obnoxious, overbearing fellow officer on board. He enjoyed antagonizing people around him who were in a position of inferiority to his "witty" brilliance. He was a real jerk and a bully. LP had only been in this new work setting for a brief time and was totally in the dark on the complex system of juvenile probation. Like all other work assignments in this organization, you learned your job by doing it. Your supervisor was your only source of light on your new task. There was no training and no break-in period.

A parent telephoned LP and explained that his son was living at home while awaiting a court appearance regarding a burglary charge. The police arrested him, and he was now back in juvenile hall. The parent was told the juvenile's case was now a bifurcated case. The parent wanted an explanation of what that meant, but LP had no idea what to tell the gentleman even though he had been assigned to prepare the probation report for the court. To say the least, LP was stumbling around on the telephone to give the parent an explanation on what a bifurcated case was. He knew that bifurcate meant to divide into two parts, but he was verbally stumbling around on the phone as he tried to give further details. His snoopy, wise guy coworker jumped on that immediately and began mimicking his sorry performance to a couple of his reluctant but amused cronies.

When LP completed his telephone conversation, he had a very urgent desire to punch somebody out. Guess who? Instead LP walked over to Mr. Obnoxious and told him he was not going to give in to his present urge and deal with him now. He told him that if he ever pulled that again, LP would have to hurt him, but he was not stupid enough to do anything at this specific time. He would resolve the matter elsewhere, perhaps in the parking lot, in front of his house, at his favorite watering hole, or at some other place of LP's choosing. The jerk wasn't any bigger than LP. He was about five foot ten, 176 pounds, and around the same age. LP figured he could handle him pretty easily.

Another coworker who was sitting nearby, broke the moment of tension by saying, "He may have looked like Clark Kent to you, Lenny, but look out when he comes out of the booth. He may be wearing a cape."

LP heard no more insults from Mr. Wise Guy, Lenny Green, but the occurrence may have become known around the department to some degree. People were sick and tired at Mr. Wise Guy's mouth and obnoxious insults to both male and female deputies. However, perhaps they also didn't want LP to come lunging at them in a caped outfit.

LP suddenly realized he couldn't spend the day dreaming away and had to get to work. He wanted to see at least ten or fifteen people today to make it worthwhile. He was preparing to leave the office when his phone rang. It was the front desk calling to tell him Wilber Schwartz was up front reporting in. Great! That was one person LP wouldn't have to hunt for today. But Wilber had come a couple of days earlier, and here he was again. It must be something important. LP got Wilber's file and ushered the man into one of the small interviewing rooms.

"Good morning, Wilber. What's cooking?"

Surprisingly, Wilber appeared to be sober. He was a hopeless alcoholic, but he was the only person LP supervised who voluntarily came into the office each month. He was one in a million. "I just wanted to report in for the month and talk to you about something," Wilber said.

"Fine, Wilber, but you were just in here Friday morning. Don't you remember?" Wilber had been completely plastered at the time.

Wilber responded, "I was?"

"Yes, you were really loaded. You could hardly talk. I told you to go home and sleep it off. You know, Wilber, you really don't have to get crocked to come in here. I'm not going to torture you or anything like that. That stuff you're getting out of the bottle is not real courage. It robs you of courage. Give that a little thought."

Wilber said, "Okay, I will, but the reason I came in today was to talk to you about something. My brother is a truck driver, and he travels all around the state because of his job. He has his own truck. He thinks it might help me with my drinking if I went along with him the next time he went out of town. I could be a lumper and help with loading and unloading. We'd only be gone a few days at a time, and I'd come in and see you as soon as we got back each time. My brother doesn't drink, and he thinks I'd stay sober if he kept an eye on me and kept me busy. You can't do much drinking when you're riding around the country, you know, especially when your brother is on your case."

"I really can't stop you, Wilber, and it might actually do you some good. But if you get into any trouble on the road, like drunk driving or anything like that, your ass is mud. I'd have to file a violation of probation on you if you got arrested and convicted for any crime or if you don't keep in touch when you get back. The court didn't take away your driver's license, for some reason, when you got put on probation."

"No, they didn't," said Wilber, "but I won't be doing any of the driving out there. My brother won't let me drive his truck. I'd just be a helper, and I'm a fair mechanic, so that might come in handy there."

Wilber was a sad, pathetic guy, and it was all because of booze. He had been in the army for a number of years and had made the rank of sergeant. Somehow or another, he had gotten busted back down to PFC while he was in the service. This was probably due to something booze related. After seven or more years in the service, he didn't reenlist but got an honorable discharge. There was no evidence that the army kicked him out for drinking or criminal conduct. He was just a hopeless alcoholic. He should have remained in the service, but he didn't.

After his discharge, he had very little or no employment and lived with his mother and brothers. The reason he was on probation was for a burglary conviction, but he really wasn't a true burglar. One night he had been walking home from somewhere—probably a nearby bar, plastered as usual—and for some drunken reason, he decided to break into a fast food restaurant near his home. He may have been hungry. The restaurant was closed for the night.

Wilber decided to climb up on the roof and go into the place through an air vent. It was a brilliant idea, but halfway down the vent he got stuck and couldn't move. He spent the rest of the night hanging there with his legs dangling from the ceiling. When the hamburger flippers showed up for work in the morning, they saw Wilber hanging from the ceiling and called the police. The fire department also had to come to the scene to pull Wilber down to earth. By that time, after a long night, Wilber had sobered up pretty much, and alcohol didn't appear to be an issue. Probably for that reason, Wilber was not ordered to abstain from alcohol by the court when he pled guilty to the charge of burglary. He was given some jail time and probation. As far as the court and probation were concerned, as long as Wilber didn't break the law, he had the privilege to drink. Wilber was really overdoing it, though.

"Wilber," said LP, "I'd like to talk to your brother about the plan. Is he around today?"

"Yes, he doesn't go out of town until tomorrow morning, and he's at home now."

"I'll go over there in a few minutes and see what he says. It appears to be a pretty good plan. Wilber," LP added, "how many times a day does someone tell you to put the cork back in the bottle? I bet you get that drill pretty often. Doesn't it get old? Aren't you getting a bit fed up with that tune?"

Wilber nodded. "Yeah, I get it a lot."

"Good. Well, let me start bugging you too. I've seen a few guys in my line of work who got tired of getting bugged by everyone and tried something different. They looked in to AA, and things got better. They got much better. You might check into that when you can. You know, it's free. Doesn't cost a nickel. You don't have to sign any papers or anything. You just show up and listen to other people shoot the bull. They don't even know your name. Everybody goes by their first name only. It's almost like hanging out in a bar with your boozing pals but without the booze. They tell me the coffee is free too. Somebody might even offer you a job. I've heard that a lot of good-looking gals go to those meetings also. I'm almost tempted to check into it myself."

As soon as Wilber left, LP grabbed his map and field book and headed out of the office. His first stop was Wilber's place. The brother verified the plan and said he would keep a close rein on Wilber. LP agreed that it might do Wilber some good. He certainly needed it.

In most cases, LP could not have cared less if a guy wanted to drink himself to death. He felt it wasn't his business. Wilber was a sorry, likable type of guy, though. LP hated to see a guy like that making his life a meaningless mess. It seemed so unnecessary. The guy had no confidence in himself, no positive self-worth, and was just slowly sinking deeper into the depths of despair. And judging from his past life, he appeared to have had a lot of abilities. He had achieved in the military and wasn't outwardly defending his present state of life. LP felt that the guy might climb out of his hole if he could move in a new direction with a little encouragement. It wouldn't work if someone else pulled him out of that hole. He had to climb out on his own. LP planned to give this a little extra attention.

The rest of the day was pretty uneventful. Early each month, LP hit the contacts with people he knew would be home. By mid-month, he would have the bulk of the caseload seen at least once. The later part of the month in the field was spent running down the people who never seemed to be home or who worked during the day. LP could generally contact the working people after five o'clock p.m. on his late days. He liked those late days because he didn't have to report to work in the morning until ten a.m. Tomorrow would be a late day. LP always made the best of those early hours on his own time. He was a kayaker, and he would head for the river and leave the world behind for a few hours.

CHAPTER 2

Two Rivers was well named because two rivers ran through the middle of the city. In a situation like that, where you were a resident and didn't have a boat, canoe, or kayak of some kind, you were, in fact, missing the boat.

LP was a kayaker and made good use of the water. Weather permitting, on weekends and on days when he reported to work after 10:00 a.m., his kayak got a bath. Between 6:00 a.m. and 10:00 a.m. was a time of both exercise and relaxation. Today, as usual, LP arose at sunup, loaded his kayak up on the roof of his car with his bike on a rear bike rack, and headed for the water. Shortly after 6:00 a.m., he was pulling his boat off the roof of his car at the river. From there, he lugged the craft over the levee to the water.

The river flow was good today. As always, he could only paddle downstream because of the current. LP's destination was six miles down the river. A slight problem was that after a six-mile trip down the river, LP would be six miles away from his car. His solution was simple. Prior to his river run, he would leave his bike safely padlocked to a large tree in a beautifully grass-covered park at his down-river destination. There was also a convenient, paved bike trail through the tree-covered, natural terrain along the river. This made the whole project work without the assistance of others.

After the trip downstream, LP would carry the kayak up over the levee to the park where he had left his bike. He would then padlock the boat to the tree and take the bike for a six-mile ride back up the bike trail to his car. He would tie the bike to the bike rack on the back of his car and drive back downstream six miles to retrieve his kayak. After locking it up, he would head back home or straight to work.

At this time of the day, there was seldom anyone on the river. One might see an occasional riverbank fisherman, but generally they didn't show up until later in the day. The area was also free of the sounds of automobiles and the city all around it. Along with the trees and brush along the route, ducks and other water fowl were always moving about. On rare occasions a few deer might be seen moving through the trees. With the exception of the sounds of the animals, the only sound that could be heard was of the kayak paddle slicing through the crystal clear, moving water. The river moved on, with or without an audience. During the salmon run in the autumn, the river would be low. A boater could look in to the clear, shallow water and see armies of the tired, struggling fish moving into the breeding areas. As the kayak moved over their path, one could almost reach into the water and touch them as they moved by.

On this particular morning, LP had only paddled downriver about a mile when he noticed a man on top of the wooded, twenty-foot levee. He was wearing a park ranger uniform. As LP paddled closer, the man yelled down to him to paddle over to the river bank. As LP paddled to the bank, he noticed a woman lying on the edge of the river, halfway in the water. The ranger waited until LP drew up and got out of the kayak.

In a loud voice, the ranger yelled out, "Have you seen any persons along the levee or in the water when you paddled down here?"

LP answered, "No persons and no activity. Not even a fisherman in sight today."

LP walked closer and took a good look at the person lying on the bank. She was a very large woman in a very colorful and gaudy dress. She wasn't moving at all and was obviously dead. There was a large, bloody wound to the back of her head.

The ranger said, "She's dead. Somebody shot her and dumped her body down the levee. They probably wanted her body to wash down the river, but she got caught up in the rocks there instead." There was a biker standing behind the ranger on the bike trail that ran along the river. The ranger indicated that the biker behind him had seen the body down there and reported the matter to him.

"I've called the sheriff's department," the ranger said. "Stick around until they get here; it won't be long. Don't touch anything down there."

LP walked a little closer to the body for a final look. It was a pretty bloody scene. He noticed that the victim had numerous marks on her forearm that might have been from cigarette burns. Based on all the blood that surrounded her, she must have been shot up on the levee and then rolled down to the river. As he walked back to his kayak to pull it further up on the bank so it wouldn't drift away, something clicked in his mind.

He yelled to the ranger, "Do you mind if I come up there? I think I know this person."

"Come ahead," said the ranger.

LP climbed the steep, bushy levee to where the ranger stood and said, "Would you believe it? I'm a probation officer and had been supervising this person until very recently. But get this— that dead person is not a woman but is a man. His name was Margareta Fred Gonzales. When the cops check under her dress, they are going to get a big surprise."

Before LP could explain further, numerous officers arrived at the scene. Immediately they began to check out the scene, taking photos and examining the body. LP explained to the officer in charge that he was a probation officer and recently had the victim on his caseload.

"I was just paddling by when the ranger stopped me. I supervised the victim briefly before he moved downtown and out of my area. His PO now is John Wills. He works in my office. I can give you a rundown on who you got here if you want. Margareta Fred Gonzales got out of the county jail a couple of months ago. In spite of those clothes, he's a man. He told me he thought he was a woman. Therefore, he ran around looking like that. He got put on probation for rolling a drunk downtown. Department A gave him a little jail time and probation.

"He got some old farmer from out of town drunk in a dive downtown and then got him up in a hotel room. The farmer passed out, and Margareta Fred grabbed his money and took off. The next morning, the old farmer woke up, probably with a big headache and no money. When he went out to a nearby bar for another drink to start the day, who should he run into but old Margareta Fred? He called the cops, and Margareta went to jail. End of story. I got the probation case because he gave the court his mother's address, which is in my area of supervision. However, he actually was staying with some other dude downtown most of the time. I had trouble keeping up with him, and the new PO has also been spending a lot of time running around looking for him.

"When I first saw him, Margareta said, 'I'm a woman in a man's body,' and I think he actually believed that. I talked to his mother, and she said, 'Yes, he's been running around in dresses for a long time.'"

LP continued, "Actually, he didn't have any criminal record we could find, with the exception of his recent offense. He grew up down the river a ways. You can see his case file and get his mother's address from PO John Wills in the West Area Probation Office.

"I think he spent a lot of his time in his mother's neighborhood because he did have some sort of a part-time job at a bargain import store near his mom's place, and he didn't have a car. But he spent the rest of the time downtown where the action was. It surprised me that anyone would hire him with the lifestyle he was living.

"It looks like somebody really didn't like him very much. I noticed somebody must have been using his arm for an ashtray. He was really kind of a pathetic person, and apparently he actually felt he was not a man. You just wonder. Life is hard enough without complicating it like he was doing. The way he was hanging around those downtown bars and acting like he was could really catch up with you eventually, and it looks like that's what happened. I wonder, though, why his body was dumped way out here so far from his mom's place and from downtown. That seems pretty strange."

The officer in charge thanked LP for the update and said he would contact John Wills for Margareta's mother's address. He said LP could take off.

LP decided to take his boat and bike home before he went to work. He was already late. Hopefully the boss wouldn't dock him for being tardy.

CHAPTER 3

On his way back home from the river, LP kept thinking about Margareta Fred's tragic end. Oh yes, he thought, *I do remember poor old Margareta*. His thoughts took him back to that memorable day when Margareta got out of jail and showed up at the office.

LP's supervisor, Jack Bothwell, dropped a case file on his desk and said, "Here's a new one for you. This file showed up in interoffice mail earlier in the day, and the probationer is up front waiting to see you."

LP opened the file, and there was nothing there but the one-page court disposition—no arrest report, no offense report, no probation worksheets, no comments or anything else. LP could see that the defendant had appeared in department A of the municipal court. That court handled the bottom rung of offenders. Most of those offenders were never sent to probation. They most often were given jail time and sent on their way.

That court handled the drunks, shoplifters, prostitutes, and other petty theft cases. They ran a constant stream of humanity through that court, and most of the offenders pled guilty on the spot and were sentenced. Every day, along with a wide variety of other matters, this court usually started out with a sad group known as the dirty dozen. However, there were often more than twelve of these drunks police had scraped up off the pavement from the night before.

If you happened to be in court to see this, you could hardly help laughing at the routine. The drunks lined up before the judge in a group and were asked individually how they pled. Generally they all replied, "Guilty, Your Honor," or "Guilty, Your Excellency," or something of that nature. Occasionally one would say, "Guilty, but with a statement, Your Honor." Then the judge would briefly listen to the drunk's lame, rambling excuse and then move on to sentencing. As a rule, if an offender had not been before the court before, he would be released from custody. If he was a reoffender, he would likely get a few additional days in jail. If the person had appeared before the judge numerous times, the court would give him or her additional time to think about things. After this group was sent on its way, the court then proceeded with the rest of the daily calendar. This was where LP inherited Miss Margareta Fred Gonzales.

LP proceeded to the waiting room and then led the lady to a small interviewing room. She looked a little unusual to say the least. She was a large person and wore a loud, long, multicolored dress that looked like a housecoat. In a word, she looked quite bizarre. She also had a large, multicolored bag on her arm. It looked like a big knitting bag. For a moment, LP felt like asking her if she worked in a circus but held his tongue.

LP spoke first and said, "You have to sign the probation order, and I'll explain what's happening and what to expect. I'll have to get a set of your fingerprints before you leave. This won't take long. Have you been on probation before this?"

She responded in a rough voice, "No, I haven't."

LP looked at the court disposition paper as he handed the probationer a pen for her signature. The printed name on the paper was Margareta Fred Gonzales. LP thought that sounded a little strange.

He said, "What's with this Fred business?"

After a very brief pause, Margareta replied, "Sir, I'm a woman in a man's body."

LP looked at her for almost a minute and realized finally that a person this bizarre could not possibly be a woman. He was having difficulty grasping the reality of it all. *What a dope I am,* he thought. *There must be some kind of sabotage going on here.*

"Just a minute, Margareta, or whoever you are," he said as he rose from his chair.

He opened the door and looked up and down the hallway. He had expected to see three or four probation officers rolling around on the hallway floor, hysterically laughing at the success of their latest prank, but there wasn't a soul in sight. It wasn't a setup arranged by wise guy probation officers. LP realized that his supervisor, Jack Bothwell, would never have been a party to such a cheap stunt as this. It was real.

LP returned to his chair and said, "Margareta or Fred or whatever name you go by, I really don't care. You can dress anyway you want, but the court has put you on probation and I'm going to be your probation officer." LP was attempting to accept the reality of the situation and wasn't angry or resistant to the way it was. Now that the facts had sunk in, he actually felt sorry for the guy. He thought, *What a life he's got. Life is tough enough without running around the way this man is. He has chosen his path.*

LP explained, "The court hasn't ordered you to pay any fines or added any other special orders. However, you will have to be seen by your probation officer at least once a month, either at home, at work, or in this office. You have to tell me if you get in any trouble with the law because it affects your existing probation status. Don't make it hard for me to see you regularly."

LP got a probation form, and they got all personal information needed. This included his residence, who he was living with, his employment, and his phone number.

Margareta said he lived with his mother and had a part-time job at an import store over on the Boulevard in the heart of LP's supervision area. He helped unload incoming goods, stacked shelves, and did other backroom jobs. LP thought, *Yes, that sounds about right. He might scare some of the customers if he was clerking up front.*

"I see your mother's address. It looks like you and your mother live right up the street from where you work. I'll be out there in a couple days to see you at home. If anything changes, you get ahold of me right away. Here's one of my cards with my phone number. Don't lose that card. Sometimes I can be helpful, but I'm not going to be your servant or anything like that. From the information you gave me, you said you don't have a car. How do you get around?"

"I take the bus or friends give me a ride."

"Keep your nose clean or you will be in trouble with the court and bigger trouble with me. The court didn't give me much information on your offense, so I'll be running down the police offense report. It will give me all the bloody details, and we can get into that at our next meeting."

LP took Margareta's fingerprints and let him go on his way. After that initial meeting, LP began to have some difficulty keeping up with the man.

Yes, Margareta, how could I forget you? You were definitely one of a kind, and now you are dead. I hope you are finally resting in peace. I think you probably earned it.

When LP finally got to work, he was a little late, but no one said anything. He told his boss, Jack Bothwell, about the events on the river and reminded him that John Wills now had the case file since Margareta had moved downtown.

The officer who now had Margareta's case wouldn't have to be looking for him anymore, and LP was certain John wouldn't grieve a great deal. Case closed.

LP had only seen Margareta twice. The first time was in the office when he signed his papers. The last time was when he tracked him down at an address downtown. After the initial contact, LP had tried to run Margareta down at his mother's place on the Boulevard. The residence was back from the street and a short distance between a trailer park and a strip mall. His mother said her son didn't really live with her all the time. However, he had a lot of his clothes and personal items there in a bedroom. He often ate at her home, but he was actually living downtown most of the time. He got his mail, if he ever had any, at her address. Her house was convenient for him because his part-time job was just up the street. She showed LP Margareta's bedroom. The closet had a lot of men's and women's clothes in it. She said she didn't have his exact address.

LP gave her his phone number and told her to have her son call him right away to give him his downtown address.

LP added, "I'm going to send out a registered letter addressed to him at your address. The letter will require him to sign for it. Don't sign it for him. He has to sign it. It will tell him to report to me now. If his letter comes back to me without his signature, I will send him back to court. If you see or talk to him, he better call me immediately or he is in a jam. It's okay if he is going to live downtown, but I have to know where he lives so probation can supervise him."

She said she would try to get to him right away; however, she didn't have an address or phone number to reach him at.

Later that day, LP prepared and mailed a registered letter explaining everything to Margareta.

Two days later, good old Margareta called LP and gave his address downtown. LP told him he would be there to see him at 10:00 the following morning. Subsequently, LP saw the man and verified that his place of residence was with his roommate downtown.

Happy days are here, again, LP told himself. Margareta was no longer his. He could transfer the case to John Wills, the PO who worked in the downtown area.

Later, after John saw Margareta, he told LP, "I owe you one, buddy, but I doubt if I can come up with anything like that guy."

LP remarked, "At least you know in advance that this character is a man playing like a woman and a cute one at that. I had to find out the hard way, by peeking, and you didn't have to. Good luck."

But now all of this was water under the bridge. Margareta was gone, and John wouldn't be supervising him after all.

CHAPTER 4

ecause LP had been delayed by the police at the murder scene and bringing his boss up to date on the big development, he was behind his schedule. He hurriedly prepared to get out into the field. While he did so, David Ally, a PO in the unit, walked into the room and said to everyone, "Hey, have you heard the latest rumor?"

"No, what's the latest?" asked LP.

"Well, it sounds like there is going to be a bunch of transfers coming down. They need some new blood in adult court and juvenile court. And they are going to be looking at any of us guys who have been in the field too long and enjoyed life too much. I heard they were going for anybody with more than three or four years in the field. I guess that would mean most of us in this unit. They are likely to take people who have done court work before. That way they can start throwing the rough court cases at them as soon as they get transferred. They wouldn't have to fool with breaking in anybody. Just strap them to a desk and load them up with cases from day one."

This was definitely not what LP wanted to hear, rumor or not. He knew he would be a prime suspect. He thought about this news. Turning out a twenty-page typed report every day of your life was not a life at all. It would stink. LP had been run through adult and juvenile court in the past, and it only brought nightmares to his mind. He didn't know what he would do if he got shoved into that again. Life was just fine where he was now. He figured that with his luck, he was as good as gone. Life was too short for this. He reasoned to himself that most of the court officers were deputy PO twos and received a bit more pay than deputy PO ones. LP had gone through all that before and was still a deputy PO one. He wondered, *If I'm considered less than a deputy PO two, why should I be stuck with that pain again?*

LP headed out in the field and began running through the list of today's contacts. As the day proceeded, he kept thinking about those hovering transfers.

For the final stop of the evening, he had a new probationer, a female adult. The court put her on probation for child neglect. She had left her two small children with a friend for an evening but didn't return for them for a number of days. While she was absent, the babysitter called Child Protective Services to report the situation. As a result, the woman was eventually placed on probation for child neglect. Currently she was temporarily camped out at another friend's residence. The court had ordered several conditions of probation, one of which was counseling. LP could see from the beginning that she was bent out of shape because the court had put her on probation. They sat down at a kitchen table, and LP explained that she had to get some counseling going. When she heard that, she immediately got all puffed up and said, "I'm not going to go to no fucking counseling."

LP looked straight at her for ten seconds, thinking of the sickening attitudes he had to deal with just doing his job. He curled his upper lip back and in a firm, deliberate voice said, "The fuck you're not." He paused very briefly and continued, "Not while I'm your probation officer."

She immediately registered a look of genuine surprise. She was at a loss for words, and LP continued, "The court gave you a break, and you don't realize how lucky you are. You could very easily lose your kids. Your kids don't need that, and neither do you. Look at it this way: in court you agreed to probation and the conditions imposed. Now you're saying, 'No, no way.' We are all in the same boat, but you are not running the boat; you will be rowing the boat. The judge is running things and will be guiding the boat, not you. If you don't row, then the judge will have you thrown out of the boat and into the water. Be aware that it might not be very restful and comfortable in the water, so you better start rowing right now.

"I'm giving you a couple of days to get something going. If you go to the welfare department and ask about counseling, they will help you. I'm sure it won't cost you a penny. Or if you don't like that and can't find something else, call me in a week, if not sooner, and I will help you find something else of my choosing. But counseling isn't something you get from a bartender or a girlfriend or on TV or from some bum. You could check with a real minister, if you know one. So get busy now.

"You were on welfare when all this happened. I suppose you are still getting help there. If so, does your social worker know where you are staying? If you don't let those people know what's going on and where you are staying, you may end up with no check on the first of the month."

LP didn't ask her for the name of her social worker because she probably couldn't even remember the worker's name. He figured he could find out himself faster than she could dig the name up out of her purse or wherever.

That concluded the friendly little meeting. On his way out, LP added, "Next time I see you, let's tone down the language a little. It affects my blood pressure and probably yours too."

LP surmised that his mouthy lady would probably run, which is the route some probationers take. They think running away will solve their problems. They go to another county or another part of their own county and try another PO. But LP felt he should really lay it on the line with her. He made it very graphic in hopes she might get the message. LP was surprised by his language and almost losing it with the woman. But at that point, he had had enough of it. He was getting to the point where he had a neck full of it. Maybe his reputation of being the guy wearing glasses going into the phone booth and coming out with his cape flapping had some merit. The lady he had just cussed out had pushed the right button to get his cape flapping pretty well.

CHAPTER 5

The next morning when he came to work, LP planned to run down the social worker or protective service worker, if there was one, for the lady he had cussed with the evening before. But first he had something more important to deal with: his future. During the night, he had arrived at an important decision. He sat at his desk in momentary thought as other POs milled around the room, answered phones, or generally shot the bull. He grabbed a sheet of paper and wrote a brief handwritten memo to his supervisor declaring that in one month, he planned to retire from the good old probation department. He read the memo over a couple times and then walked into his supervisor's office, grabbed a seat, and handed Jack his memo.

Jack read it and said, "This is extremely unexpected. What's going on here?"

"I can't say I have any logical answer to that, but if you've got the time and want to put a couple nickels in me, I might figure it out for both of us. If I run off at the mouth too long, just tell me to compress it. That's what I've wanted to tell a lot of people we see every day. They sometimes rattle on forever and don't say anything I need or want to hear. This idea has been on my mind for the past few days, and the more I've let it roll around my mind, the more I like the idea."

He continued, "Last night I think things came to a head. I had a home contact with a new female probationer, and I did something I've never done before. She's on probation for child neglect and has court-ordered counseling. I told her that's what the court ordered her to do, and I could give her some suggestions to get the help. Well, her exact response was, 'I'm not going to go to any fucking counseling.' I thought about it for a few seconds and then I said, 'The fuck you're not. As long as I'm your PO, you are going to get the counseling you were instructed to get.'

"When she heard my curt response, she about laid an egg, I think. She just blinked. I'm sure she was totally surprised that anyone could treat her like that, just the way she probably treated everybody else. She didn't say much after that exchange and started listening to what I had to say. I told her about a few places she could pick from but that she had to get going on it now. But from the limited experiences I've had in all these wonderful and fruitful years, my guess is she may take off with or without her kids and make it hard for everyone, especially her children. I explained that counseling wouldn't kill her and that it's free and would allow her to keep her kids. I added that her children didn't deserve to be shafted by some bad decisions on her part."

Jack didn't say, "Compress it," but listened without comment, and LP continued. "Last night after work I began to realize that I'm not able to remain detached or ignore the attitudes of many of these people anymore. I could have told her what most POs would have suggested she should do. They would say, 'If you don't want to get counseling, then don't get counseling. It's your decision. If you go your route, you will be violating a condition of probation, and you will be sent back to court. Then the court will make its decision.' Most POs don't saddle themselves with other people's messed-up lives. They just do the job the court and the probation department assigned them to do.

"Just yesterday I was talking to another probationer who has a bad drinking habit. I took on my social worker pitch. I suggested he check out AA, which is a fitting suggestion, but I almost volunteered my own time to drag him to an AA meeting myself and give him a little added support. I should have said, 'There's AA available. Look into it or don't. Your drinking is your problem. Don't make it mine too.'

"For a long while, I've had the growing feeling that the PO gets pushed around by everyone in the system, including the people on probation. We get the thankless job of making the justice system run smoothly for the court, the judges, the cops, our bosses, and everyone else, and we, the drones at probation, get damn little. And that could be somewhat true. But you know what? Last night I also realized that the system doesn't care one way or another about me. The system doesn't owe me anything, so I need to quit expecting something. If I want to feel sorry for myself, I can stick around and blame the system. It's my decision to make. When I decided what to do, I felt very relieved. I'm a free man. I feel great.

"And to heck with all the rumors. We've been hearing the big rumor about transferring a lot of us lazy bastards out of the field and rewarding them with a soft job in the court. I've heard my name was included on the list. I'll be cutting them off at the pass. I don't think the system needs me that bad. I'll be quitting while the quitting is good and attempting to salvage as much of my life as I can."

LP realized he had run off at the mouth for more than his nickel's worth, but his mental relief was so great that he couldn't seem to shut up. Jack was a good listener. LP continued.

"I've got a lot of years in with the county for retirement, but I don't intend to take any money out until later down the road. I was looking for a job when I started here, and I've had a lot of other jobs. I'll find something to do somewhere and survive somehow. You have been one of the very best bosses I've had in probation besides being a friend. And I thank you for that. I've had a lot of good bosses and I've had a few bum ones too. I'm sure you can say the same thing about all the boobs you have had working for you.

"All of this made me think of something I read a while back. Let me bore you with it while I'm on my soapbox, and then I'll get out of here and earn my pay. There was this Greek philosopher named Heraclitus who said, 'No man ever steps in the same river twice, for it's not the same river and he's not the same man.' And he was so right. That's very profound thinking and can be chewed on for a long time. It's a heavy statement that says so much in such few words. There were a lot of philosophers in the past, and they made a lot of sense. This guy lived back about five hundred BC. That's five hundred years before Jesus Christ. You don't find that kind of genius coming out of world leaders these days. Now it's mostly smoke and mirrors.

"Heraclitus said that the only reality is change and that permanence is an illusion. All things carry with them their opposites; therefore, being and not being are in everything. The only real state is one of transition. Heavy stuff, isn't it? Anyway, I guess I'm just going with the river and headed for a little change, good or bad. The longer I hang around here, the more it feels like I'm standing in quicksand, and it only took me a couple months to come to that conclusion. I hope you let me work for about three weeks longer until the end of the month. That way I can get all this month's work cleaned up for the next guy. I won't dog it. I'll try to keep in focus to the last day. After that, I'll take a real break for a while, maybe head for Lake Tahoe and the water. I've been saving my dough and have a little in the stock market. I've also collected a few coins over the years. Coins aren't worth much now, but you never know about gold and silver. It goes up and down."

As LP got up to leave, Jack said, "I don't like seeing you leave us, but I know you will do okay wherever you are. I'll send your memo to the big boss. They will probably send somebody to take over your caseload. Hopefully you'll get some time with whoever it is and can show him or her how it works."

LP went back to his desk with a feeling of complete relief. *It's over,* he thought. *My bridges have been burned, and there's no going back. A month from now, it will be no sweat.*

CHAPTER 6

The next day, LP's supervisor told him they were going to bring in his replacement very shortly. He'd been working in juvenile hall and had no other probation experience. He knew nothing about field supervision.

How fortunate for the new guy, thought LP. Field supervision was very simple. *After about three weeks with me, I'll have him totally educated for this job.* More often than not, when someone got assigned somewhere, the prior tenant was long gone somewhere else, and the new guy was left twisting in the wind without a clue. A lot of the old-timers loved watching the new turkey suffering through the maze and were not about to lend the guy a hand.

LP decided he would dump as much of his own self-discovered wisdom on this new guy as possible so he might bypass some of the numerous pitfalls that are out there. He wished others might have done the same for him. A few good souls had come to his aid and pulled him through, and he was grateful for that. At least the new man wasn't going into court at this point.

LP decided to get out in the field early and round up as many people as he could so he could coast toward the end of his last month.

As his day progressed and contacts were made, his mind wandered. Most of the officers he had worked with were great people and were easy to get along with. Most of the supervisors he had were also professional and excellent. But some of them could be otherwise. You might say that many were implementers while a few were impeders. He had worked with each type, and he had survived both. They came and went.

Among the implementers, LP remembered one supervisor, Ralph Lee, who was very skillful in his approach. He let the POs do their job and respected their decisions. He'd often be seen reading the newspaper. Ralph was a real hillbilly type and had no ego problems. He knew his job. He lived on a few acres of ground on the edge of town. He grew all kinds of vegetables and even had a tractor. He'd occasionally bring big bottles of pickles to work, and you'd see him munching on them at his office desk. He probably grew and canned the pickles himself. LP figured he probably played a fiddle and went to square dances and things like that. LP never asked him, though.

LP remembered a day when he got a new case and a man came in to sign his probation papers, as ordered. As LP began to explain the conditions of probation and what was expected of him, he briefly listened and without notice, said he didn't want him for a PO. He wanted a different PO.

LP told the man, "Okay, that's fine with me. But somebody is going to have to be your PO. I'll get my boss to help out and see what we can do."

When Ralph got the message, he said, "Fine, we'll go up and see him. We'll fix him up." LP had no idea what the result would be.

In the interviewing room, Ralph said he understood the man wanted a different PO and agreed that something could be worked out.

"All of the POs are at maximum caseload right now," Ralph explained. "So the only thing we can work out right now is that I will be your PO. How does that sound to you?"

The man loosened up and said, "That sounds fine to me."

Then Ralph said, "There is one small problem. I have to stay in the office all the time to provide direction and supervision of POs assigned to me. I can't go into the community monthly to make contacts. The only way I can supervise you is for you to come into the probation office. In a case like this, you will have to come into the office regularly, about once a week, which would probably be acceptable to the judge." When the fellow heard that, he appeared stunned.

He said, "You mean I have to come in here four or five times a month?"

The boss said, "That's right. Doesn't that sound fair enough?"

The man replied, "No. I'd rather have the regular PO come out and see me at home."

The boss rose to leave and answered, "Okay. Mr. LP Cinch will be seeing you at home then."

End of conversation. Later in the day, LP remembered he'd thanked his boss for the brilliant offer he'd made to Mr. Smart Guy.

Ralph commented, "He won't last long before he fouls it up somehow."

LP remembered saying, "I agree. My guess is it'll only take two months, at the most." Sure enough, they were right. The man moved out of the area two months later and probably gave some other PO the job of chasing him around. Ralph Lee was a real class act.

On the other hand, LP thought of another supervisor he had later on who was a genuine company man. This guy thought he was the only one who could do the job properly. He was constantly in everyone's caseload, offering stupid suggestions and directives. You could tell he was driven to get a promotion by driving his underlings to perfection through his stupid plans and interference. He could be listed as a definite impeder. He micromanaged every caseload and appeared to feel that everybody working under him was stupid, ignorant, and untrustworthy. It appeared he believed he was the only one who knew how to do the PO job. His actions suggested that he thought the POs wasted their time in the field through failed planning.

At one point he instructed the workers in his unit to keep a daily written log of the time spent in the field. The record would show the time the PO left the office, the time of arrival at the first stop, the time the contact was concluded, the time it took to go to stop number two, and the time the PO spent taking a leak, if necessary. LP had included that item in the interest of total accountability. The officers spent their entire day filling in the little squares on his form as they journeyed around the city each day. The boss probably thought they were driving out of their way to make contacts instead of scientifically laying out their movement to save time, but there is no science to know when people will be home and when they won't be.

On occasion this supervisor would ride along with a worker when he went in the field. LP remembered that he rode along with him on only one occasion, fortunately, and it turned out to be a very enjoyable event. On that day, when he found out that he would have the boss with him for the day, he picked a lot of contacts he knew would be home in the morning and early afternoon. He also wanted to be selective and possibly set some sneaky traps for the boss. LP was hoping get him to question why he did things a certain way. He might even come to realize that his way wasn't the only way. Everybody and every PO generally worked a little differently but possibly just as efficiently as the boss might execute the task. LP thought he might even get him to realize that the poor peons might do all right even without the help of a lot of his wisdom.

One contact they tried to make was on a young man LP had earlier supervised when he was on juvenile probation. He had been released favorably from probation but was now on probation again, this time out of adult court, though. As a juvenile, he had never been a problem and never gave any sign of being involved in anything illegal. However, now it appeared that there might be something different going on. He was supposed to be living in a large, seedy apartment complex with this mother.

As they drove to the complex, LP explained to the boss that he had been there earlier in the month and nobody was home, so he left his card with a note on it that the kid was to call or come to the office for an update on things. LP also mentioned that he had heard a rumor that the young man could be mixed up with a bunch of people who might be involved with drugs.

The complex had only one entrance and one exit. The layout was like a big U, with the entrance and exit at the open end of the U. The complex was two stories high, with apartments on both stories. Tenants and visitors could park on either interior side of the U. Usually most of the parking spaces were taken.

When they arrived at the address, LP didn't drive into the complex. He parked his car outside of the complex on the city street. He figured that the boss would question why he did that, and he was right.

He asked, "Why don't you drive right into the place?"

LP said, "Oh, for several reasons. For one thing, that entrance is the only exit, and I just like to play it safe at a place like this. Also, when you've been to a place like this a few times, driving that same car, the residents, who are no dummies, catch on pretty quick that you are either a social worker, parole officer, probation officer, or cop. Before you get out of your car, everybody in the joint who has anything to do with you almost instantly knows you are there. As a result, they get everything out of sight that they don't want you to see. Or maybe they just don't come to the door when you pound on it. Who knows? But if they don't see my car, I just briskly walk in from the street and I am at someone's door before they know what hit them.

"I'll give you another reason. Remember that cop that was shot over in Elm Park less than a year ago? He was shot while driving around in that area. They later got the juvenile gang member and his two pals for doing the shooting from a second-story window in an apartment area there. Well, a short while ago, the police got wind of a possible plan to pull the same thing at this place—to shoot another cop. Nothing happened, but you never know."

LP thought he would try to put the boss on the spot. He continued, "What would you do if you parked your car in front of someone's apartment, and after talking to your party, you came back to your car to leave and some big, beefy gorilla was sitting on your car fender while talking to a couple of his evil-looking pals, and he says to you, 'I want your battery'? How would you handle that?"

The boss pondered momentarily and said, "You could show him your probation badge, I guess. What would you do?"

"That's why I park out here. But if I parked inside and that happened, I don't think I would wave my badge in his face. I'd be facing him and his two slobbering buddies. I'd be a little outnumbered. I'd hate to have to come up with a good answer to the question asked by the doctor when he asked me, 'How on earth did you get that badge up your ass?' That's one reason I usually keep that thing out of sight. About the only time I really have to show it is when I have to see somebody in the county jail. This guy lying on my car thinks he's funny and tough. He wants to show off in front of his pals. Go along with the gag, and try to make him look a little silly at the same time. He knows who I am. I don't have to show the badge.

"I'd probably say something like this: 'Well, friend, I'd like to help you out, but this isn't my car. The car belongs to the sheriff's department, and I can't just give you their battery. It's not mine. I can call the sheriff and ask him, though. Who knows? He might okay it. He might even send a couple of squad cars out here to help you get the battery out of the car."

LP continued, "By jiving and amusing them a little, you might escape without a scratch and still have a battery. Also, I find that if you give people choices, they feel less threatened and usually make the most sensible decision. Don't argue, but give a choice."

The boss said nothing for a minute or so and said, "Yeah, I guess you're right."

"There are several other reasons why I park here, but I guess you get the idea," said LP. "Also, people don't like to see people like us coming up to their front door when all of their neighbors are looking out of their windows to spy on them. Would you?"

We exited the car, walked into the complex unobserved, and knocked on the apartment door. The kid's mother came to the door. He wasn't home, but at least the parent was there. She said she didn't know where he was but confirmed that he did live with her. She confirmed that he had a part-time job working for a man on the river trapping crayfish. They sold them commercially, but this was a bad time of the year and things were a bit slow.

LP explained to the mother, "Your son is giving me the runaround. You tell him I want to see him either here or in the office before Friday. Frankly, I'm worried about him. In the past when I supervised him on juvie probation, he was always available, and he never seemed to be messing up. Do you know what I think? I think he's messing around with drugs and druggies. I want so see him pronto. We all have to get on the same page and right now."

When we walked out of the complex toward the car, LP remembered saying, "Well, what do you know? Nobody is taking a nap on the hood of my car. Some days you just get lucky." LP wanted to get more contact in before the lunch break and decided on one that might be interesting.

As they drove to their destination, LP gave the boss a preview of the case. They were headed to the home of a female probationer who was guilty of possession of marijuana. She was living alone with two small children. She and her husband were separated, and he lived in another part of town with his relatives. They didn't live together because it would affect what they would receive in welfare. If he was a resident in the home, he would be required to participate in the work project. He was jobless and on probation for a different crime. He had a different PO. LP surmised that before her conviction, the husband was hanging around her residence a good part of the time and the marijuana rap fell on her when the weed was found in the house. He had probably been selling dope, and word got around. The police came and found the dope when he wasn't around. He skated on that rap at her expense. He had probably convinced her not to implicate him in the crime because he was already on probation at the time, and it would have been very bad for him to get another conviction.

When they got to the lady's address, LP wanted to impress his boss with some dramatics. When they were admitted to the house, he walked over to the stove and opened the oven door. There was nothing inside, of course, and he said, "This is where she was hiding the dope."

They hung around very briefly and started heading out the door when the boss glanced out the kitchen window into the large backyard and saw a big doghouse in the far corner of the yard. You could almost hear the gears grinding in the boss's brain.

He said, "Did you ever check that doghouse? That's a good place to hide something."

The woman volunteered that you had to go into the garage and out the side door to get to the backyard. LP remembered that at this point the gears in his own head were doing a little grinding also. He was standing behind the boss and facing the woman. He noticed that she was about to say something further, but she didn't speak because she saw LP giving her a no signal as he shook his head.

The boss said, "Let's take a look" as he headed to toward the garage. With the boss leading the way, they proceeded to the side door in the garage. The boss was feeling his oats and was hot on the trail. He was about to crack this case and catch this gal with the goods. He didn't know it, but with a little luck, he was going to make LP's day.

The boss stepped outside and headed toward the doghouse. In about two seconds, a huge dog came charging straight at him. The dog was growling and quite upset, with slobber dribbling from his mouth. It was a grave intrusion upon his turf. Fortunately for the boss, the dog came to an instant stop in midair. The dog was at the end of his rope just a couple feet short of the boss's face. The boss looked like he had seen a ghost and quickly retreated backward as LP yelled, "Buster, get back. Get back!" The dog stood his ground and continued growling.

The boss seemed to regain his composure a bit and said, "Well, maybe you can check that doghouse another time. Let's let it go for today."

When they got safely back in the house, the boss asked the woman, "Why do you have a dog like that?"

She said, "It's not my dog. I hate it. It's my husband's dog. The only reason it's here is that he has no place else to keep it. I have to feed it and everything else."

The boss made the comment, "That animal is a menace. I would keep it tied up at all times."

LP also said, "I don't know how often you see your husband, but don't let him drag you into any of that evil weed. It's your place and your neck. Put your foot down. Explain that to him."

As they were leaving, LP requested the use of the restroom and proceeded down the hall while the other two remained talking at the front door.

As they left the house, the boss said he had decided to get back to the office for the rest of the day. As they drove there, LP apologized for not warning him about the hound in the backyard.

He said, "I knew they had a dog from earlier, but I thought the husband took him someplace else. I had no idea he would still be here today."

The boss commented, "I noticed that you knew the dog's name."

"Yes. Whenever any of these people have a dog, I always get his name and remember it. If you can call dogs by name, sometimes they don't act that hostile. I also usually record license plates and car descriptions. Stuff like that comes in handy all the time.

"Anyway, we learned a little something today, even though it doesn't make any difference one way or the other; it's just a little extra information. I think we know the husband is very likely hanging around part of the time. When I asked to use the bathroom, I actually checked the closet in the master bedroom. I wanted to see if any of his clothes were in the closet. There appeared to be no men's clothes in sight. But we do know he is around some of the time."

The boss asked, "How is that?"

"Because his dog is here. This guy may abandon his wife, he may abandon his kids, but he would never abandon his dog. So he's around."

So went a memorable field trip with a memorable boss. Shortly after the mad dog incident, the boss told everyone in his unit that they could cease keeping the silly travel records. LP also noticed that the boss cut back on a lot of his confusing drills. He was eventually transferred to another assignment, so working obstacles faded away.

Now here he was, back to the present and down to his last few days as a PO. LP planned to see as many people as possible before turning the caseload over to a stranger.

Even though he griped to himself and whoever else he could gripe to about his job, the job had been a real education along with keeping bread on the table. And some of those days, like the day his boss had almost tangled with that vicious dog, would forever be remembered as one of the very good old days. A little prank now and then can go a long way toward cheering up the troops. The best part of it all was that LP figured that the boss had suspected he'd been set up that day.

At the time, LP was prepared if the boss raised the question of trickery on his part. In the face of such an accusation, he could avoid repercussions by falling back on a real hard-rock defense. He could say, "Boss, you're smart enough to know that I am too stupid to stage such a stunt as that." And of course, the boss would have to agree.

CHAPTER 7

Several days after Margareta was killed, LP received an early-morning telephone call from a probationer. Earle Swope asked if LP could he come out to see him. He said he had a problem and didn't know what to do. This was a rare occurrence. People hardly ever contacted their probation officers regarding their problems.

What on earth could Earle need help with? LP figured this must be something pretty important. He knew Earle had no telephone and most likely didn't have the dime to spare on a phone call.

LP asked, "What's so important? This better not be some wild goose chase. I just saw you a couple of days ago, and I'm a busy man."

Earle responded, "It won't be. I can't tell you on the phone, but it's about Margareta. You know her, don't you?"

"Yes, I do. I was her PO. Do you know she's dead?"

"Yes, I know that," Earle replied. "We read it in yesterday's newspaper. That's why I'm calling you, but I can't talk to you on the phone."

"Well, sit tight. I'll swing by your place in about an hour. Be sure to be there."

At times LP figured some people needed to be enlightened as to the limits of the PO's duties. People got the misguided idea that the PO was going to be their pal or something. Occasionally he had to boil it down to the cruel fact that the PO wasn't going to be their social worker, caddie, shrink, cab driver, banker, or you-name-it. Unfortunately, however, contrary to his big speeches, he often crumbled one way or another and treated them as they should be treated: like human beings, imperfect creatures like himself. But friend or foe, LP always tried to convey that when the judge said you have to do certain things to remain on probation, it's up to the PO to verify and record it. If the offender didn't do anything required by the court, the court wanted to know. If there was a problem, it was the offender's problem, not the PO's.

Earle's shack would be LP's first stop for the day. When Earle had mentioned Margareta's name, LP immediately knew this was something that must be important.

He wondered what Earle would know about the fate of poor old Margareta. But everybody on the boulevard seemed to know what was going on out there. Word travels fast. Earle wasn't too swift, to say the least, but LP had ears, and Earle did like to blab.

LP headed out to Burke Boulevard, which was the center of his working territory. It was referred to by the surrounding residents as the boulevard. Long before the world of freeways, this road was a major highway entrance from the west into Two Rivers. With the coming of modern freeways, this route was reduced to a moderately busy city street. In earlier times, it was made up of busy motels, travel parks, small restaurants, gas stations, small grocery stores, used car lots, and numerous other stores and shops. Used tire shops and animal feed stores were included too.

Over the years, it took on the appearance of age and neglect. However, it remained a busy section of the city for the people living around it. Many areas along the road never had sidewalks, and as a result, the pedestrians, who were many, walked along the edge of the street. There were no Macy's, Sears, or fancy restaurants. The places of business, for the most part, remained what they had been before and since World War II. The few modern, well-known establishments included Kmart, McDonald's, and the Colonel.

Many of the people living there worked for the railroad or in one of the many canneries. Most had lived in the same homes since birth. They were honest, hardworking people. This wasn't the country club part of the city. There was an atmosphere of harmony, and most of the people knew their neighbors and the shop owners. Among them were also the people who could get into trouble. LP was supervising a good part of that group. And just as there is crime and criminals on Wall Street and elsewhere, there was also crime on the boulevard. Fittingly, this was where Earle Swope resided.

Earle was an interesting, likable guy, and like many, he was not any big threat to society. He was on probation for stealing tires from the screened backyard of a second-hand tire store on the boulevard. Later he attempted to sell the tires back to the people he had stolen them from—a less-than-brilliant move. They recognized their tires and figured out what he had been up to, so Earle ended up on probation. No one else convicted of the offense because Earle was alone when he attempted to make the sale. His two roommates were most likely involved, though. Earle, the good soul he was, didn't snitch them out. But LP figured they were also involved because the three of them were nearly always together.

Earle and his friends lived in a small shack very near the tire shop. He was often unemployed and was getting financial assistance from the county. He was quite young and seemed to have some sense, but it was limited, probably because of past drug use. He may have even attended college at some point in his past. LP believed Earle was an ex-hippie but had never inquired on his past. At this point, Earle and his friends were reduced to a life of cheap wine and easy living.

The friends were a young woman and a young man, both of whom seemed to have fewer remaining gray cells than Earle. It appeared Earle was in charge of thinking for the group and made all the big decisions. It was obvious there were few decisions to make because every day was a holiday for the three—four, including their dog.

Very often when you drove along the boulevard, you could see the three of them walking along the road with their very large mongrel dog, which was named Biff. Biff was led around at the end of a very large rope tied to his hairy neck. They collected aluminum cans and checked Dumpsters along their way. They appeared to be quite compatible with their casual lifestyle. LP wondered what would be the result if the household group took an IQ test to see who was the brightest. LP figured that if he were a betting man, he would put his money on Biff, but it would be close because you could see that Biff was no genius either.

Their residence was situated behind a small mom-and-pop grocery store. The store managed to remain in business because the owner let people have credit when they couldn't pay. He owned several small shacks behind the store, which were occupied by very low-paying renters. They could best be compared to small chicken coops. They had no heating and limited lighting. Each consisted of one room. An outhouse was shared.

Because of the two small beds, there was little space to move in the enclosure. When LP contacted Earle, he usually just stood inside or talked to him outside. He had a fear of bugs.

"We were looking at Friday's newspaper and saw that Margareta got murdered," said Earle. "And we've all been scared since we saw that. We've been thinking that whoever shot Margareta is going to come and shoot us too."

"Why would anybody do that?" said LP. "And who is going to do this shooting? I saw the article in the paper too. She got about five or six lines and that was all. They have no idea who killed her and have probably buried her case file under fifty other cases. They more than likely sized it up as a couple drunks fighting over a bottle. Working on that one would be like looking for a needle in a haystack."

"We think the mob will hunt us down and kill us."

"The mob? Come on. Why would the mob be after you folks?"

Earle said, "About a week ago, I think it was either Friday or Saturday, after we ate dinner we were going down the street to get a jug at the liquor store. We were getting low on wine. It was almost dark, and we were walking along. We saw Margareta walking toward us on the other side of the road. You can always notice her because of those dresses she wears, you know."

LP interrupted, "Yes. She sure was a knockout in those outfits, wasn't she?" LP was grinning, and the others all chuckled.

"As we were getting close to her, she stopped. She stopped, I guess, because there was a cop car slowly coming up the street from behind us. I'm sure Margareta saw them coming. They drove by us and past Margareta. They drove up the street about a block and a half further and started to make a U-turn. Margareta was watching them, and when she saw that, she quickly looked around. She was right in front of the used tire place, and she walked over toward the front door where there is a stack of tires about four feet high on each side of the front door. She took her purse off of her shoulder and dropped it into one of the stacks of tires there. I'm sure the cops didn't see what she did. When the cops drove back past us, they parked. They waited until Margareta walked ahead toward their car. When she got close to their car, the officers stopped her and talked to her for a minute or two. Pretty quick they put her in the back of their squad car and drove off."

"Why would they pick her up?" asked LP.

"Maybe to just give her a hard time for being around. I think they knew she was on probation and wanted to shake her up a little. Maybe they just wanted to do something besides drive around all night."

Earle went on, "We waited a while and then we went across the street, and I reached down into the stack of tires and pulled out her purse. It was big and heavy. We figured somebody else might get it. We thought it was best to take it home and give it to Margareta when she got finished with the policeman.

"After that we went and got our jug and then walked home. The bag was heavy and full, but we didn't look into it until we got home. We guessed it was probably some of her clothes and shoes and stuff like that.

"We waited for Margareta to show up, but she never did. We thought we might get a reward from her for saving her bag. But then we saw she'd been shot, and we really didn't know what to do then. We decided to call you, but by then it was the weekend, so we called you today."

LP said, "Let's clear up this mystery. Where's the famous bag?" Earle dragged out the bag from under one of the beds and placed it in front of LP, who was standing near the door.

LP's curiosity was killing him, and as he bent down to look in the bag, he commented, "What the heck is in that ugly bag anyway?"

"It's what might get us all killed," replied Earle, "or maybe make the cops think we robbed a bank."

LP looked in the bag, and there it was. He sat down on one of the beds, bugs and all, and dragged the bag in front of him. He dug down into the large bag, looking for any kind of note or written message or a gun. There was none. The bag was full of paper money in bundles. He removed one bundle of hundred-dollar bills and closely examined several of the bills. They weren't counterfeit. They were the real thing.

After his examination, he looked up at Earle and the others and said, "This is unbelievable, but I hope none of us gets killed over this."

He looked back down into the bag again, and after a brief silence, he mumbled to himself the answer to his own question, *What the heck is in that ugly bag anyway?*

His answer was the famous punch line he had heard long ago in one of his favorite Humphrey Bogart movies, *The Maltese Falcon*: "It's the stuff that dreams are made of." LP added, "And that could get us murdered."

Dashiell Hammett was the author of the novel *The Maltese Falcon* in 1929. It was later made into a movie in 1939 and starred Humphrey Bogart, who appeared as Sam Spade, private eye. Toward the end of the movie, the cops are marching away the crooks and murderers to jail after they've tracked down a large statue of a falcon. This black bird was supposedly made of solid gold, but in this case, it was a fake made of lead. A police officer examining the falcon curiously asked Bogart, who had cracked the case, "What is this thing anyway?"

Bogart's response was, "It's the stuff dreams are made of."

That statement was the highlight of the classic movie, helping it to be acclaimed as one of the all-time greatest pictures in the film noir category.

However, if you were to read the novel, you would find that the statement was never written by Dashiell Hammett. It ain't in the book. It is *not* in there, friends. Hollywood added that statement in the film and put the cherry on the top of the sundae, so always read the book.

LP had roughly counted the bundles of hundred-, fifty-, and twenty-dollar bills in the now-beautiful bag. There had to be close to fifty thousand dollars all told. They appeared to be all used bills. There were no consecutive numbers.

CHAPTER 8

L P didn't know what to say next. *This is a mind-blowing deal,* he thought. He had planned to see a lot of people today, but it looked like that plan just went down the tubes.

Earle's tale appeared to be completely believable, but LP had to ask one more time. "Earle, are you certain the three of you didn't rob any bank?"

"No, Mr. Cinch, we didn't rob any bank or anybody. There ain't even any banks around here if we wanted to."

"Good point," said LP. "Where did she get this kind of money? It must have involved some kind of drugs, but I'll get back to that in a little bit. Let's review what you know about Margareta. This happened about a week ago. Did you see her again after the evening the cops picked her up out on the street here?"

All three shook their heads and gave an emphatic no.

"Have any of you said a word or talked to anyone about any of this business?"

Once again they all gave LP an emphatic no.

"That's good. That's excellent. You all get an A-plus on that one. If anyone gets wind of any of this, I fear it will be curtains for you, so don't say a word. However, you could just call up the cops and tell them to come and get the whole bag of money. Just wash your hands of it. Forget it and walk away from it."

Earle quickly said, "No. If it's the mob's money and we did that, the mob would come kill us just to get even. We thought that if we could give the money back to the mob, they would be happy and wouldn't come kill us. They might even give us a reward. But if we tell the police, they will probably think we killed Margareta to steal the money. And who would believe us? Nobody. The only way is to find the mob and give them the money."

LP said, "I think you are way off the track about this mob business. There's no mob around here that I ever heard about. Maybe bikers or some gang like that. Anyway, if you want to hold off on calling the police for a few days, I guess it wouldn't make that much of a difference.

"Let's get back to Margareta. If this is a drug matter, she couldn't handle anything of this size. This is a major thing. I doubt if she had any connections. Rolling drunks was her speed, nothing like this deal. I doubt if she had any money to deal with an operation of this size. Had she been throwing around any money in the neighborhood lately?"

"No," said Earle. "But we asked her if she could spare any change a couple weeks ago and she gave us a dollar. She was nice that way. But I don't think she made very much money working at the import store. She only worked there about half the time or less."

"I'm sure you're right about her finances, Earle, and that's why I'm of a mind that she had to be working for someone else. The main crook was using her for a mule. She was working for someone who didn't want to stick their neck out on some sort of an exchange. They figured they'd let Margareta take the risk of getting caught with the drugs. A big question is, if it was drugs, was she selling or buying?"

The money. What about all this money? LP thought. *We have to figure out some plan on that right away. We have no idea where we are headed here.* He felt like walking away and letting them screw it up on their own.

Finally he said, "In a way I tend to agree with Earle. Giving the police the dough is not the best plan—at least not yet. We haven't any idea what went down. It could have been some legitimate deal. But once the cops get a hold of it, you will never see that money again. It will disappear, gone-o."

Earle said, "Yes, let's give it back to the mob and go for a reward."

"Well, first we have to put a lid on it," said LP. "You don't want to tip anybody off like the cops or the mob by spending a lot of money around here. If the mob goes for your plan, it could go good for all of you. But if the mob finds you with the money before you talk to them, they are likely to plug you now and ask questions later. It could be that Margareta got caught in that squeeze, and we see what she ended up with."

LP added, "I don't think you should keep the money here because somebody might come snooping around and catch you with it. If you want me to take the money and stash it someplace where it will be safe, I could do that. And then I could ask around and find out who the money belongs to and go from there. What do you think about that?"

All three nodded their heads in agreement and said yes.

LP warned his little group, "Listen, if I do this, you will have my neck sticking out a mile. Do not mess it up. Not a word to anyone. My ass is on the line here. Don't you dare rat me out."

LP continued, "Now back to the drug part of this. We all agree that Margareta was not a big dealer with the organization to do something like this, was she?"

Everyone agreed on that.

LP said, "She had to be working for someone. That's the only thing that makes sense. But who would that be?"

Earle volunteered, "Well, she worked for John Richards at the import store. His wife actually owns it. She's from Vietnam, I think."

LP listened to Earle and realized something startling, almost unbelievable. He had Earle on his caseload, he had Margareta on his caseload before she moved downtown and got killed, and to top it all, he also had John Richards on his caseload. John was on probation for receiving stolen property. LP had a good many of the probationers in this area, but to possibly have three of the people tied up in this deal seemed astonishing. He knew Richards' wife had a store in the area, but he didn't realize it was the import store. He remained silent and listened to what Earle was saying.

"Since it's an import store, it seems like they could be sneaking drugs in with all those imports. And Margareta had been helping out some people around here when they needed drugs real bad. She wasn't doing a lot of that, but I heard she had been doing it sometimes."

"That looks like a very good prospect to check out," said LP. "I'm going to take off now. I have a lot of other things to do today also. I'm going to take the money and stash it. I'll get back here as soon as I have some news—hopefully good news. Now remember, squealers and blabbers get cops and robbers, and you don't want either group in on this. Don't even talk to each other about this. And don't go doing anything on your own until you run it by me. I don't want to be blindsided, and I'm sure you don't either. I'm going to go over and take a peek of that tire shop right now."

On his way to the tire shop, he had to admit to himself that he was back on the wrong side of his job again, just like he had told his boss. He was acting like Mr. Social Worker again. He was acting like he was an arbitrator, a fence, a counselor, a conspirator, and everything he had said before. The sooner he dumped this job, the better. He hoped he could get out of this before he also became a cellmate of the three he just left.

He parked on the street near the tire store. It was an area with no sidewalk, just a dirt trail next to the road. He walked up to the front door of the place and noted the two four-foot-high stacks of old, worn-out tires. There was a chain looped through each stack. The chain was bolted to the wall for safekeeping. They didn't appear to be worth stealing. He looked into the interior of each stack. All he saw was a Popsicle stick in one; no more bags of money today.

Margareta certainly was a clever one doing her dance step to the tires when she saw the cops closing in on her. If they had stopped her with that bag of money on her, she would've had a lot of explaining to do. She would have been a goner. She was lucky but not completely lucky. You might say Margareta was close but no cigar. LP's three stooges came along and torpedoed her plan, and she ended up in the morgue. Margareta's mother looked like she couldn't finance a burial and all that went with it. LP would have to look into that and perhaps put his social worker hat on one more time before he bid good-bye to his job.

He wanted to get the money stashed somewhere before he did another thing, so he headed for his place. He decided the best place for the swag was in one of his kayaks. He kept the two of them suspended from the ceiling of his garage. It was a task to get them down, and probably that fact would discourage most burglars. The boats were a sit-on craft with a large, covered storage compartment behind the seat. At the stern area of the compartment was a small cavity with a door that would be just the right size to contain the bag of money. That was where LP put the bag to rest.

When he finished that job, he decided to go back to the office and do some paperwork. Among other things, he wanted to check in on Mr. John Richards, store owner and possible dope peddler. There might be some clues in his file.

CHAPTER 9

pon his return to the office, LP's boss notified him that his replacement, Donald Lamond, was joining them the next morning.

"Let him follow you around for a few days, and clue him in on all your secrets and shortcuts. He will do fine with your guidance. He will be in and out at first because he still has a few things to finish up on from where he was. He's only been working in the hall for a couple of years."

LP wanted to work on the John Richards matter but decided it was time to compile a list of the dos and don'ts of this job as far as LP was concerned. He would list every minute thing on keeping your nose clean. It would be a list of the thousand things nobody told him when he started this job.

LP decided to type out this gem and borrowed a typewriter from the steno pool. He began:

Know where the best restrooms are in the field.
Fast food restaurants aren't bad, and there are several
public libraries in your area. They're very good. If you

want to kill some time out there, the libraries are the best for catching up on your notes, to find a phone number, or whatever. Nobody will see you in there if you are just loafing around.

Don't be running around in grocery or department stores on company time. That's a no-no.

You can tell the probationers in the field that you just want to see their faces each month. It will put them at ease, but actually you want to see everything else that matters. Keep your eyes peeled.

Don't give any employment recommendations. You never know when your man is going to rip off his boss.

Don't provide any transportation or money because you aren't a cabbie or a banker.

Be friendly and concerned but distant. Let them know that you have only one boss, and that's the court.

Don't take any gifts of any value.

Don't choose sides with any probationer or relative. They will start playing you like a Ping-Pong ball if you get in the middle of their games.

See as many people as you can very early in the month. You can see them more often if you have the time.

Record any license plate numbers, dog's names, names of relatives, if important, and phone numbers.

If they have a job, don't mess it up by seeing them at work if that would cause a problem. In some cases seeing them at work is no problem and works well for everyone.

Get your monthly report to the boss very early in the month. Don't be spending all your time doing last month's report when you should be out seeing people this month.

When in doubt, go to your supervisor; that's what they're here for. They want to be in on things.

Don't record anything you can't back up.

On court appearances, don't take a lot of files and records with you. Take just what you need. Lawyers love to get their noses into your field book to see if they can shoot you down in some way. Also, don't volunteer information. Just answer questions that are asked.

Don't rock the boat; you are only a passenger.

Don't be afraid to say no out there. Probationers are very good manipulators. They're experts at it.

Don't pass on defendants' information at the request of people other than the court, other probation people, or the law. Don't give bill collectors any addresses or do their work for them. You can pass on information to the probationer, if requested.

Play it safe at all times. When in doubt about something, get advice from your superior. It's better to go down in flames with the boss than by yourself if anything goes wrong.

At all times, cover your ass. (I will give you a couple of examples on that issue.)

Please burn this after reading it. You didn't hear it from me. It's all bologna any way you slice it.

At the conclusion of his monumental written monologue, LP decided to prepare another typewritten item that would be given to his three mob-fearing friends on his next trip.

Next he directed his attention to the probation file of John Richards. The man was on probation for receiving stolen property and served a brief jail sentence in the county jail. He was a civilian employee of the air force and worked at the local air base as a mechanic or technician. At times, as a part of his job he was sent out to Pacific air bases to do mechanical work of some kind. These jobs were in the Philippines, Japan, Korea, and elsewhere in that part of the world. His wife was from Vietnam and owned the store on the boulevard.

Regarding his criminal offense, he showed some lack of good sense in that he pawned an expensive piece of jewelry and provided his name, which is required. He received about five hundred dollars, approximately half of the true value, which is normal. He apparently didn't know that all pawn shops monthly provide a complete record of all these transactions to local law authorities. They traced this item back to the burglarized victim and had their man. It doesn't pay to be a dumb crook. LP thought about the crime and theorized that Richards didn't appear to be an active burglar. But if he was selling drugs and someone offered him the jewelry for a meager amount of drugs, it might make a nice, tempting profit for him. And when caught, he certainly couldn't say he got the jewelry in a drug sale.

LP planned to give this some serious thought, but now he wanted to check something out about Margareta. He wanted to talk to Margareta's mother.

Even though Margareta was dead and his probation connection was now zero, LP wanted to see Margareta's mother, Delores, on a secret mission. Before that, he made three brief contacts with others on his caseload. This would justify his being in the field. These people got the "I just want to see your face" treatment. All appeared to be doing as expected by the court. Now he could go see Margareta's mother. When LP arrived, Mrs. Gonzales was home alone. She said she remembered LP, and yes, she was grieving but managing.

LP said, "I'm here because I didn't see anything in the newspapers about Margareta's burial services in the obituaries, and I was concerned. What happened on that?"

"My son's body is still at the county morgue. We aren't sure what we can do about the burial. It's a big expense for me and all my relatives."

"I thought that might be a big burden," agreed LP. "That's why I came by. I've come up with something that could help everybody with this burden. Let me explain and see if you would be interested.

"I know of a group of church people who like to help out in extreme cases like this. They have helped me out before. They consider this a kind of religious calling where they help out with money in cases of need. The important thing with them is that they must not get any credit or notoriety for their charity. I guess they think that if they get any credit for this deed then it isn't true charity work. Any true charity has no name. They want to remain nameless, so if you accept their help, you will be asked to allow me to be a kind of middle person. You give me the details, and I am expected to arrange everything. I will receive money, and I'll pass it on to everyone involved."

"Oh, Mr. Cinch, that would be the answer to all my prayers. I can hardly believe this is happening. This would be a miracle."

"Okay, Mrs. Gonzales. Give me some details, and I will make all the arrangements. But part of this agreement is that you can't reveal my involvement to anyone. The only thing you can tell anyone is that you were contacted by a charitable group who said they wanted to assist you but wishes no credit for recognition. Actually, if my name got known, I could probably end up in trouble at my job. I might even get fired, so you must not mention my name to anyone. Okay?"

"Yes, whatever you say, Mr. Cinch. I agree to keep my silence."

"First I will contact the county morgue and tell them you want your son's body to be released and that the body is to be taken to a mortuary, which I will contact to receive his body. I will let you know the name of the mortuary as soon as I make arrangements with them. Do you want funeral services, and where would you want Margareta buried?"

Mrs. Gonzales said, "Most of Fred's relatives are all buried at the cemetery in Pearburg. And we have been going to St. Thomas Church in Pearburg. It would be nice if we could have services at St. Thomas."

"That can be done," said LP. "I will contact the people in Pearburg and make arrangements. Let me tell you how this is going to go, hopefully. First I will make arrangements with the funeral parlor to prepare Margareta. I will select a good casket. Next I will contact the minister at St. Thomas for a date for the services. I will contact the cemetery and arrange for a plot and a gravestone. I will notify all of the persons involved to call you with all information on dates and times. I will arrange with the mortuary to provide you with transportation to and from the church services and burial if you need it.

"Now I need some information from you. I assumed you wanted a regular burial, but maybe you would prefer cremation. My church people will pay for either."

"I don't think we would want him cremated if he doesn't have to be."

"That's fine. What name do you want to have on his gravestone? Margareta Fred Gonzales?"

"We would prefer Fred."

LP got her phone number, exact address, and all the other needed details and requested some clothing for Fred. She provided a man's suit and shoes.

LP said, "I'll take the clothes to the mortuary. I will contact everyone involved and take care of all the costs. I will give them your phone number and direct them to follow your instructions. I will instruct them to send you receipts of all the costs of the work they will do. I will leave you with my phone number, but call me only if you need help. After today you are to make like you don't know me. Don't let me break my bond with those generous souls with their financial help, and don't mess me up with my job. I'll deny ever talking to you. If you don't have transportation on any part of this, call the mortuary and tell them."

As LP was leaving, Mrs. Gonzales appeared very uplifted and said, "All my prayers have been answered. My son will be put to rest in a way I never dreamed. Fred didn't really have a happy life. In school all the other children used to make fun of him. But he was a good boy and a good son. Thank you so much."

"Don't thank me. Thank the church people. I will tell them you are very, very happy with what they have done."

LP thought Margareta deserved this sendoff and at the expense of the rats who killed him. *We will dip into that bag of cash and not spare the horses.*

He also realized that he had volunteered a large amount of money from that bag of cash. That meant he had gone from spectator to totally involved and in the center of a potential bull's-eye. He had to pray for a lot of luck and cover his ass. There was no going back now. He had to go get some of the money and then head to the mortuary.

CHAPTER 10

LP's first stop after seeing Mrs. Gonzales was a quick trip to his place to get some cash from his kayak. The famous purse was right where it had been. He had to do some quick math and decided to take mostly hundreds but a few fifties and twenties, totaling about seventy-five hundred smackers. That should get things rolling. Hopefully he wouldn't need more.

While LP drove to the mortuary, his thoughts raced. For so long, LP had felt like a rotting log in the forest. However, with these recent events, he felt more like a man running the one hundred-yard dash, and there was no finish line up ahead. Since he had decided to dip into the money, he fully realized he was no longer in the audience. He had become a serious actor on the main stage.

Somehow his conscious mind wasn't accepting that new decision, but at the same time, his subconscious was telling him to do otherwise. His subconscious appeared to be making decisions that his conscious mind didn't accept or fully understand. That deeper mind was taking him for a ride, but he didn't know to where. It was also telling him on the way to cover his ass, hang on for the wild ride, and add some defensive plays along the way. Perhaps all of this might partially avenge Margareta's death. On this little journey, he had to move fast and not look back because they may be gaining on him.

At the mortuary, LP explained to the gentleman in charge that he was assisting an anonymous group in an act of pure charity. All the costs of assistance would be handled through himself on their behalf. He realized he had to explain with caution. The funeral director was less likely to swallow his tale than Mrs. Gonzales. It probably was a rare occurrence for a group to come up with such a large amount of dough without some sort of personal gain or recognition. LP had to explain very carefully and not allow the man to smell a rat. He went into detail on the need for anonymity for the group and for himself. Without that, they could do no business. Perhaps when the man saw a handful of hundred-dollar bills waving in front of his eyes, any doubt or curiosity would vanish.

LP recited the explanation he had given Margareta's mother earlier and added that he would be paying the full amount in cash. He directed the man to prepare an estimated cost of all the necessary procedures, including the cost of a casket. He explained that Mrs. Gonzales would probably need transportation to and from the funeral and the burial site in Pearburg.

He emphasized that he and the charitable group would remain anonymous and let today's cash speak for itself. He sweetened the pot a bit and explained that his group planned to be involved in future similar projects, and based on the good performance of his mortuary, they would certainly return for more assistance.

LP requested that he be given a receipt for funds given today and said he wanted a written summary of costs to be given to Mrs. Gonzales upon conclusion, along with any cash balance. The services were to be held at Saint Thomas Church in Pearburg, and Mrs. Gonzales would notify them when the services would be held. Regarding the gravestone, the funeral director told LP he could work out that matter through the Pearburg cemetery and church.

The director presented a list of costs for caskets available and an invitation to personally inspect samples in another room. LP looked at the list of seven options and costs. He indicated that a personal viewing wasn't necessary and selected casket number three.

After a brief pause, the representative summarized the total cost and passed the paper for LP's inspection. LP removed an envelope from his jacket pocket and began counting out that amount plus two hundred dollars.

This man and this type of business organization were the helpers of the world with noble, admirable goals in a world of grief, but like all others, they are normal humans. When they hear the customer say, "It will be cold cash in advance," they seem to betray their containment.

LP thought to himself, *I wish I was rich. I haven't had this much fun in a long time. When they see you counting out a stack of green paper with $100 printed on each sheet, you can almost see the drool on their lips.* He wished it would happen to him sometime in the future. *I would be the drool champion.* Any piety in the room would appear to be kicked into the corner when evil greed peeks in the window.

LP detailed the whereabouts of the body and said all further arrangements would be conducted between the mortuary and Mrs. Gonzales. However, the charity group would be examining all aspects as the work proceeded.

LP was surprised by how little time it had taken to complete this part of his big plan. He would have to officially take some time off from work tomorrow and head for Pearburg on a church matter. But today he had time to squeeze in another little job of importance. He needed to rent a letter box at one of the city's branch post offices. He didn't want to get a box in the zip code where he lived or in the zip code where Margareta had dumped her purse. He selected a different branch near the mortuary. He got himself a box. He hoped he would shortly get some answers, but he might not get any answers. Either way was fine, but this would help him in the cover-your-butt department, he hoped. From here he headed back to his good old job on the boulevard.

Without a specific list of people to see, LP decided to concentrate on ones who lived or worked close to the boulevard. Probationers could often be a good source of information if they wanted to be. LP figured he would find out if anybody knew anything about Margareta without making anyone suspicious as to his special interest in the murder. Finally he hit on one guy who knew who Margareta was. He was at his job working in a cheap shoe store near where Margareta had dumped her purse. He was on probation for possession of drugs and appeared to be doing well. He had been working steadily and was supporting his wife and kids. LP had tested him regularly at the office for any sign of drug use, and he had no problems there. He was always a good contact for LP because he was at work every day. After discussing the shoe business briefly, LP eased in to the matter he was most interested in.

"I was sorry to see that one of your old girlfriends got bumped off about a week ago, Freddy."

"Very funny, LP. I guess you mean Margareta. Listen, I'm a happily married man. Don't start any big, fat rumors. Margareta was something to see strutting up and down the street, but she seemed harmless. Nobody deserves what she got. She wouldn't hurt a fly. I saw her out on the street a couple of days before the report in the paper. It was kind of funny because it was right after ten in the morning, right after I got to work. She was walking up and down the street like she was lost or something."

"Do you suppose she was looking for something maybe?"

"Could have been. Anyway, that was the last time I saw her."

"What day was that? Do you remember?"

"Wednesday or Thursday."

That's about right, thought LP. Margareta was out there the morning after the cops picked her up. That must have been the last time anybody saw her except for the killer. LP speculated a bit. After the police let Margareta go, she came back for her money, but it was gone. She very certainly panicked and took off. She knew they would be displeased with any tall tale she would lay on them—even mad enough to plug her. Losing the money would put a pretty good dent in their wallets. And of course, they would not have wanted the word to get out that they had just gotten ripped off to the tune of fifty grand. Whoever lost the money wrote it off when they rubbed Margareta out.

A little later in the evening, LP picked up some very pertinent information from another person he was supervising. He could always find Clyde Lombardo, who was on probation for petty theft, at the local bowling alley on the boulevard. He worked there part-time doing odd jobs like cleaning the restrooms and vacuuming carpets. The rest of the time he was there with his friends. LP checked him off for a monthly contact and then brought up the subject of Margareta.

"It was pretty bad news about Margareta getting bumped off, wasn't it?"

Clyde replied, "Oh, did Margareta get killed?"

"Yes, didn't you see it in the papers?"

"No. The only thing I read in the paper is the funnies."

"She got shot, and somebody dumped her in the river about a week ago."

"She was around the bowling alley a lot of the time. She was always walking because she didn't have a car," said Clyde. "I remember she was out here in the parking lot about a week ago. It was pretty early in the evening, and she was talking to some guy in a brand-new Chevy Corvette. It was a black convertible. What a beauty. You don't see many of those things around. That's how come I remembered seeing her there in the lot. I was sitting out in front having a smoke. You wonder why a guy like that would be hanging around talking with Margareta."

"What did he look like?"

"That's what was strange. He was a young guy, a lot younger than Margareta, and well dressed. They were talking there when

I went inside for a Pepsi, and when I came back out, they were both gone. Boy, that was a real nice-looking car."

LP assessed what he had just heard, and things began to connect. The bowling alley was only three blocks up the street from the tire shop. Margareta's mother's house was two blocks further down the street, and a couple blocks further takes you to the import store. Margareta was either headed home or to the import place when she dumped the money. If that was the case, it meant Margareta had already completed the transaction. That meant that Margareta was the seller of something and not the buyer.

And something else to boggle the mind was the car; a brand-new black, convertible Corvette. They were few and far between. Mostly you saw them in the front window of the new car dealerships. *And by golly,* LP said to himself, *I just happen to have a guy on probation who has one like that.*

LP shook his head in disbelief. *If my man is involved, then it would seem that almost everybody I am supervising is mixed up in this murder. Margareta was on my caseload before she transferred out, Earle Swope, who found the money, is mine, John Richards of the import store is looking like a murderer and drug dealer, and now we add another to our gang. That would be Ray Linn, who is also on my roster. Things like this just don't happen—or do they? I guess they do now. If you add me to the mixture, that makes five of us. Four alive and one departed. We could start a basketball team.*

CHAPTER 11

When Clyde Lombardo mentioned seeing that black convertible Corvette, LP knew where he had seen one just exactly like it. Ray Linn would fill the bill exactly. It was unbelievable. LP had just recently gotten the man on his caseload. He'd only seen him on one occasion. He didn't live in LP's area but he got him because another PO was overloaded. He was living in an area of more recently built homes. It was a little more middle-class territory than LP's turf.

LP had wondered about him from the start. He had gotten out of the military a short while back after serving out in the Pacific and Southeast Asia for a while. He had been living in Southern California. He came up to Two Rivers to explore starting a business of some sort, but he didn't say what type of business. While he was in Two Rivers, he was put on probation for being in possession of a sawed-off shotgun—slightly illegal, to say the least. But what was really fishy was that he had a very nice Harley Davidson motorcycle in his garage. He also had nice furniture in his place and some expensive-looking paintings on the walls. They were Oriental, along with everything else in the place. This guy had to have hit a jackpot somewhere to live like this without a job. He had just recently gotten out of the county jail after serving a few months for his conviction. LP had figured that the court must have given him a break on the jail sentence because of his military record. Or maybe he had a very good lawyer. Maybe he had a little pull from somewhere.

But to add to all of these questions in his mind, one other thing raised big red flags in LP's mind. Getting in to the man's house was a huge problem. His residence had a small porch at the front door. Around the exterior of the porch was a metal grill. To get into the place, you had to ring a doorbell and enter only when someone inside released the lock on the door. It looked like a large cage. This wasn't a usual arrangement in some parts of the city. Old people and people who feared being robbed often had something similar on their houses. But you didn't see any places in that neighborhood with a similar setup.

This did look a little fishy. LP didn't dwell on the appearance of the place when he had made that initial contact because he guessed Mr. Ray Linn just didn't want to get his place ripped off. But now he had second thoughts about why there was so much security. He would have to talk to his boss to see what he might think about it.

When LP arrived at work the next morning, he was greeted by his replacement, Don Lamond. Don was a young, athletic-looking guy who looked like he had just won first prize in something. He was all grins. LP could tell right off that he must have been looking forward to his new job. Great!

As he sipped his coffee, he told Don to take a seat. Two other POs were in the unit early and were getting organized. LP introduced everybody and then turned to Don. "After being in juvie hall with all those wild juveniles, you're going to love this job. It's so entertaining; it's like going to the movies. Just don't volunteer to be part of any of the performances."

One of the other POs, Brett Woodman, joined the conversation and asked, "How come you're quitting your job, Cinch?"

Alvin Cohn added, "Yeah, Cinch, what about that?"

The word that LP was quitting had traveled fast around the building, and of course, the main topic was what would become of LP if he quit. Would he starve to death? Would he die of boredom?

LP decided to embark on a bit of levity to start off the day and to have a little fun. He said, "This is something I had to do. The little gray cells in my brain are so bruised and battered that I can hardly function anymore. This job has burned them out almost completely. I need a job where I can earn a little dough to keep afloat and that will allow my brain to recover, if possible. There are a lot of jobs that require zero brain functioning. I've given serious thought to relocating to Nevada or Monte Carlo, several of my favorite playgrounds. I could get a job in a casino making change. You've seen those guys walking around in the slot machine area of the casino who make change for the suckers. All they have to do is stand around with fifty or one hundred dollars in nickels hanging from their necks for eight hours a day and keep the gamblers in change. Now that's a job I could do standing on my head. Absolutely no brain work required. It's like recess all day.

"Or there are the seasonal jobs for those who like sports. I could be a sweat scraper, a no-brainer, and you get to see the games for free."

"What's a sweat scraper?" asked Don.

"A sweat scraper? Haven't you seen those guys who stand at each end of the basketball court? Whenever a player falls on the floor and gets sweat all over everything, the sweat scraper rushes out with a rag or a brush and mops up the sweat. And he has the best seat in the house. It's seasonal, of course, but again, no brains required.

"If you like the outdoors, you can always check out the tennis tournaments and get a job racing out on the court to retrieve runaway balls so the game isn't delayed. Of course, that's seasonal. But again, you get a ringside seat for the action."

LP's audience showed signs of tiring, but he pressed on. "There's all kinds of work out there like that. Every casino in Nevada has a lot of restrooms. Providing paper towels and occasional mopping is another no-brainer. And if all others fail, there are hundreds of jobs as pearl divers in the restaurants. I already have a wealth of experience there. I was in the army, you know. I picked up a lot of valuable skills-skills that are life lasting and there to fall back on. I was very skilled in peeling potatoes, and I excelled in pots and pans. Those army cooks won't allow any grungy cooking tools."

His audience was now dozing off, but he forged on. "On any of those jobs you go to bed at night and know you will be needed and appreciated the next day. And there's no deadlines, no unfinished work when you go home at night, and no one constantly messing with your poor old gray cells."

LP looked around and said, "OK, now everybody wake up and get to work." Brett and Alvin dispersed immediately, but there was no escape for the new man, and LP would start loading him up with all the wisdom he could scrape up. He started out with the lengthy dos and don'ts he had typed up earlier in the week.

He tried to put Don at ease and said, "This is just a lot of garbage you've heard before, I'm sure, so don't consider it as any ten commandments or guiding star. I was just killing time when I wrote it. I doubt if it even makes any sense. Like I said, damaged gray cells. Our supervisor won't be in until later today. He is the best. You'll like him. You can rely on him whenever you're stuck on anything."

"I can only be here until noon," said Don. "They told me they need me at the hall in the afternoon today. Also, they told me I will be in and out for the first week or so."

"That will work out fine, especially today because I needed to take off at noon today myself. I have some personal stuff to do. Maybe we could just grab my field book and run out and see a couple of people till noon. You'll see how simple this job is."

Before they could leave, LP was informed that a new customer was waiting to be seen. LP looked in his inbox and found the folder. The boss had dropped it in the box the day before.

"Before we leave, we can see this man and you can see how this works. We will have him sign his orders, explain everything to him, and take his prints. Then we can head out into the field. This won't take long."

LP scanned the file before he saw the man. He was on probation for vandalizing an automobile and got some jail time, probation, and restitution to be paid to the victim—his ex-girlfriend. He was from the Bakersfield area and worked in the house-building business. He had jobs in the Two Rivers area before his conviction. He had signed the probation order while in custody and was directed to report here upon his release from jail.

LP told the man, "You have two probation officers today, myself and Don Lamond." As he gestured at Don and handed over one of his cards, he said, "Don't lose our phone number. It's important. You will be seeing Don after this month. I'm being transferred. If you move or have any changes, call one of us or come in here and see us. If we lose track of you, the court will issue a bench warrant because of that. If you head back to Bakersfield or wherever, be sure to let us know. A warrant hanging over you would mean that the cops would hold you in their jail until you end up back here in front of a very upset judge. Who is this you're staying with now?"

"She's just a female friend," he responded.

"What are you using for transportation to get to work or whatever?"

"I have a motorcycle. It's parked outside. Since I just got out of jail, I'm between jobs right now."

"Mr. Lamond and I will come out and see you in a few days. Maybe next week. I need to take your fingerprints today, and then you can go. I hope you can get some work. There is plenty of construction going on around here."

Don watched LP take the man's prints, and they sent him on his way.

As LP and Don exited the office to make some stops in the field, LP commented, "I wouldn't be surprised if your new man is gone before we check on him later. I told him we would see him soon because he looks like he has no anchors hanging on him in Two Rivers."

"Why is that?" asked Don.

"In spite of my going on and on about warrants, he looks like he thinks he can outfox the world. He has a new girlfriend after messing up his ex-girlfriend's car. He's working home construction, and there are jobs all over California and Nevada. Many of these guys go from job to job. He is free as the breeze with his motorcycle. What's to hold him back? He can leave Two Rives in his dust. We'll check him out, and my guess is we'll be sending his file back to court before the month is over. I hope I'm wrong but that's life. If he takes off, I can show you how to file all the forms on a violation request."

As they spent some time knocking on doors in the field, LP decided to pass on a little cheap wisdom. He started by saying, "I gave that long, boring list to you to read. I think the last item I wrote was about the most important. It was, 'Cover your hind end.' That one is the most important for you personally. Probationers have relatives and so-called friends who are always ratting on the guy who's on probation. These people want you to punish our guy because they are mad at him or something. Parents of kids on juvenile probation are the worst, but we get adults a lot also. They call up and say so and so did this or that and what are you going to do about it. You're supposed to go and get in the middle of their lives. A lot times that is not necessary, but there are other times when you must take action or it could blow up in your face. Let me give you a classic example that happened to me very recently.

"I have this old guy on probation for drunk driving. He lives with his wife, and he is an alcoholic. One condition of his probation was that he was to abstain from all alcohol. In this particular case, the wife calls me and says her hubby is drinking at home and he took the car and went to some bar on the boulevard to have a few more rounds. The thing here is that this guy's problem has now become my problem also. Some POs might dismiss the matter and let nature take its course, but the fact is, if this knothead gets in a car wreck or runs over someone, the wife can say she told the PO what was going on. And she's right. The situation has to be resolved one way or another or the PO could be the chump. It had to be dealt with right now. Not later.

"In this case, I grabbed my hat and drove over to the area of his house. There are numerous bars on or near the boulevard. The best thing to do is start checking the ones closest to the knothead's home. It's probably a place he hangs around in all the time. I had a description of the guy's car and his license number, which is the first thing I record when I get a case. Sure enough, at about the third place I checked, called the Squeeze In, I spotted his car in the parking lot behind the bar. I went into the dinky beer bar. You could tell that the half-dozen barflies sitting on barstools at the bar probably spent most of their lives in the joint, and knothead was one of them. He had a half-full bottle of beer gripped in his hand. There was an empty barstool next to him, so I sat down next to him. I said, 'Hi, remember me? I'm the PO that explained to you that there is no drinking while you are on probation. Now you are in trouble, and you are making a lot of work for me. I have to send you back to court. I have no other choice. Your judge is going to really be on your case.'

"I couldn't tell if he was drunk, partly because he never said a word while I made my speech. However, I now had a more immediate problem: his car was in the lot. I couldn't let him drive it home or anywhere else. He could get in a wreck on the way home. If that happened, I wouldn't have solved anything. I could drive him home if he would cooperate or call his wife from the bar and tell her to come get him. Fortunately, the bartender came to my rescue. He walked over and said he would take his car keys, which he did. He said, 'We'll get him home.'

"Oh great, I was off the hook. When I got back to the office, I called the man's wife and explained everything to her. After that, I prepared the papers for the court. A week later, at the hearing, the judge put the guy back on probation. No jail, no nothing. The guy had a smart lawyer who got the guy's doctor to say that because of the man's medication, he was somehow confused or whatever and not responsible for his violation, so he got a free pass. But the probation officer didn't because the court ordered the PO—that's me—to submit three-month memos to the court relative to the man's progress. Out of all of this, I covered my bottom. That's what you need to do when something like that is dumped in your lap. He is one of your people now."

After seeing a few good probationers, they headed back to the office and called it a day. LP had personal things to do after lunch.

After lunch, LP contacted the grieving mother one final time, he hoped. He gave her instructions and phone numbers to complete the burial. Amen.

His next stop was to the local newspaper, where he wanted to run an ad in the lost-and-found section. After his recent snooping, he had a pretty good idea about the origin of the sack of money. Still, he had yet to come up with a solution on what to do with it. His plan had to show some sign of an effort to return it to its rightful owner. Usually if a person loses his dog, he checks the lost-and-found section in the newspaper. If someone was looking for Margareta's stash, they would probably do the same thing. LP's ad could work as bait, but it also could show some effort on his part toward returning it to its rightful owner. That person would be a killer, a crook, or both. The last thing LP wanted was to have the money traced back to himself or to Earle Swope and his friends. It would all be transacted through the post office box he had just rented. The three-day ad purchased by John Founder read as follows:

> Money Found. Provide me with your identity, the
> amount of money, and the general area where it was

Jack Mannion

lost. If you can do that, the money is yours. Mail to
PO Box 79, Two Rivers, 88442.

LP had one final thing to do, and it would have to be his best
performance of the day.

CHAPTER 12

n his way to see Earle Swope and company, LP made a quick trip at a local bank to get one of the last hundred-dollar bills he had raided from the stash broken down into five-dollar bills.

When LP got to their place, all three were sitting on the small porch of their dump. Their dog was snoozing with them. Earle appeared happy to see LP, as usual. Immediately, he asked about the money.

"I have some good news," said LP. "I got lucky and ran the man down that we were looking for. I told him I knew some people who found your money and they want to give it back to you. I think he is part of the mob. He was surprised and happy to hear that. I didn't give him your names or tell him where you live. I told him I had to get your permission first to do that, but I did give him the money. He said he wanted to give you a reward. I told him there were three of you who found all that money, and he said he wanted to thank all of you. Also, he said he didn't want anything to get the law tipped off that the money even existed or that any crime was committed. If that happened, he said his boys would be out to see you about that. You wouldn't be able to hide from them for very long.

"He gave me this letter to give to you," said LP as he pulled the envelope from his pocket and handed it to Earle.

Earle hastily ripped it open and pulled out a thin stack of five-dollar bills.

"Wow," said LP. "How much have you got there? It looks like a hundred dollars or more. Oh, there's a letter there too."

As Earle counted the money over and over, he said, "Read it to us, Mr. Cinch. You were right, it's one hundred dollars."

"Okay, hand it to me and I'll read it.

> To my friends,
>
> Thanks for helping on this deal. From now on we figure you to be our friend. If you keep your trap shut, we are gonna send you some money every so often, maybe once a month, for being our friend. If we give you a whole lot of reward all at once, somebody might get wise and make you squeal. If you did that, we would have to come and rub you out, so don't double cross us or we will squash you. The money we will send will come from different towns because we move around a lot. Your pal that talked to us will also have to be rubbed out if you screw this up. Remember, keep your trap shut or it will cost you big time for sure.
>
> Your new friend,
> Al Capone Jr.

Earle continued to shuffle the bills around as LP said, "It looks like you have a good start now, Earle. You and your friends never told me what you are living on here. Have you got any money coming in?"

Earle said, "Phil gets a check every month from the county because he is disabled, and so does Barbara. I work some days at the car-wrecking yard taking parts off of wrecked cars. They just tell me to come in when they get some new wrecks in or when somebody else quits. They pay pretty well. We also collect aluminum cans and some junk. And we get some food every week from two churches."

"If Barbara and Phil get aid, doesn't someone come out here to see you?"

"Oh yes," replied Barbara. "She is always asking why we don't move somewhere else. She comes out here about every month. We tell her we don't want to leave here. We like it here just fine. We don't pay hardly anything for rent, and Leo, the grocer, lets us work for him sometimes in the yard or in the store. He cashes our checks too. And he doesn't bother us. He even lets us use his phone, but we don't call much."

"Well, it sounds like you don't want to change things for now. If that money starts coming regularly in the mail, it's got to help some. All you have to do is sit back and act like the three little monkeys. I'm sure you have seen those little statues of the monkeys, namely see no evil, hear no evil, and speak no evil. That's all you have to do. Anyway, you know who Al Capone Jr. is, don't you?"

"I think he must be Al Capone's son," volunteered Earle.

"I think you're right," continued LP. "Back in Chicago they called the old man Big Al. He died in prison, but he ruled Chicago. One time some other crooks tried to muscle in on his action. He invited about ten of those guys to his warehouse to talk it over. He lined all ten up against the wall and machine gunned all of them. The cops never did anything about it. Maybe they were scared of him. Think about that. He was bad.

"Now here is a possible problem. I will have to give Al Jr. your names and address; otherwise they won't know where to send your reward money each month. Is that okay?"

"Yes," responded hear no evil, see no evil, and speak no evil.

LP explained, "If you move, you will have no way to contact him with your change of address, so you've got to stay right here or the letter will go to the dead letter office. If you move, you might be able to get the letter if you go to the post office and give them your new address. You won't be able to come to me because I am leaving my job pretty soon and the guy who takes my place knows nothing about this deal. It could get real bad for you guys if he finds out. Okay?"

LP got another affirmative response from the three. They were totally on board.

"Now, you do have a mailbox and you do get mail, right?"

"Yes," said Earle, "our mail comes to the store. The exact address is thirty-nine sixty-one and a half, cabin three, Redding Boulevard. The only mail we usually get is the county checks and some junk mail. The address of the store is Victory Market, thirty-nine sixty-one Redding Boulevard."

"I'll pass this address on to the man. Now don't mess this up, and the dough will keep coming."

After LP left them counting their five-dollar bills, he attempted to analyze the recent moves. Good or bad, smart or dumb, the money was still waiting for a home, and almost all of it was intact. Nobody apparently was claimed it, and even the three little bears rejected it. No one knew where the money came from. No one knew if it was part of some sort of crime. There had been no arrests, no nothing. As far as the world was, concerned the dough never existed, and it was likely that it was almost impossible to unravel what happened. Margareta's death hadn't been solved or connected to any other crime. She had handled the money, but that didn't prove any crime had occurred involving the money. LP reasoned he could tell the three finders involved to go ahead and call the police, explain everything, and turn the money over to them. Could the police relate the money to any crime? Doubtful. It was certain, however, that if the authorities got ahold of that money, no one would ever see it again. It would be swallowed up in the bureaucracy and put to rest there. Of course, how kind and deserving of them to keep it for themselves.

Or LP could support something even more out in left field. He could return all the money remaining to the three stooges and tell them to take it and get lost in the crowd. He could imagine the result. They might leave the dog behind, hop on a bus to Disneyland, and leave a steady trail of money behind them. Who knows what would result from that bunch walking around with wads of money falling out of their pockets? That would definitely lead to John Law galloping in with troops wanting to find out how they came up with this unbelievable wealth. Poor Earle and his chums would never again be able to recapture their current state of contentment. How could anyone disturb that state of Utopia those three and Biff were living in? That would be a real crime for sure.

Today LP had no answer. He was stumped for now. Answers had to come from somewhere. At least he had stabilized things for now with Earle and company. The gang bought the whole fairy tale, and they loved it.

When he got back to the office, he had several phone messages to take care of. One looked important. Sheriff's Officer Hal Schaefer wanted him to call back as soon as possible. *Uh oh. What does he want? Better call right now.*

Moments later on the phone, Hal Schaefer said, "Thanks for returning the call. We understand you are supervising a man named Raymond Linn. Correct?"

"Yes sir. He is one of mine. What do you need?"

"We are planning a search of his place," said Schaefer. "We're preparing a warrant. Can you tell me a little about where he lives?"

LP answered, "Yes, I sure can. I'm glad to hear you're planning that. I've only been to his place once, and after looking around the place a bit, I was thinking about calling someone to share what I saw. I wasn't sure where to start. I was wondering if I was overly suspicious or what. First of all, he's driving a new Corvette. He's got an expensive-looking motorcycle—a Harley—in his garage. He's got no job that I'm aware of. You know he's on probation for possession of a sawed-off shotgun, and he just moved up here from Southern California before he got caught with the gun. There's something very interesting if you plan a surprise search. In that case, I'd suggest you take along a wrecker.

He's got one of those locked metal cages around his front door. The only way you can get in there in a hurry would require pulling that thing off the wall."

LP added, "He's living with a female adult and apparently nobody else. I didn't see a dog around there. I could guess, but what would you be searching for?"

"We have information that drugs are involved."

"Well, you know he likes to play around with guns. I didn't see anything like that when I was there, but I didn't conduct any search. Like they say, where there's smoke there might be fire. This guy didn't act like any dummy. He looked like a guy who likes the finer things in life, and because of the way his house is furnished and all the gadgets he has, it appears he's in the money somehow. How would I find out if you find anything?"

"I'll call you back if we go out there with the warrant. If we find what we suspect, you can look to find him in the county jail since he's already on probation."

If they raided the guy's place and found drugs, it would definitely answer the big question of the day in LP's mind. It would mean for certain that Margareta was selling the drugs and her transaction had been completed. She was going back to her boss with the swag. The drug buyers, namely Ray Linn and friends, got what they were buying and weren't involved in any murder. Why would they be involved? They had paid their money and gotten their goods. The person who sent Margareta out didn't get his money, and he didn't like that. He was the murderer. You could put in in the book. And so who was the big boss? Who didn't get his money?

LP had to check something out. Ray Linn had just recently gotten out of jail on the gun charge, and John Richards also had recently finished his jail sentence for stolen property. Could it be possible that these two knew each other because they were both sharing the sheriff's hotel at the same time? Could they have met in there and made business plans while in custody? It was very possible. LP could dig up things to confirm that, but he knew a shortcut to get the answer easier and quicker. It could be just a waste of time, but it would satisfy his curiosity if he checked it out. Fortunately, he had a friend who worked in the county jail. He was a social worker assigned to the jail to assist the jailers with resolving minor inmate problems relating to welfare, family problems, and things of that nature. With the presence of a social worker in the jail, the jailers were relieved of the endless stupid problems inmates could cook up while in custody. They could be told, "Just tell it to the social worker." Fortunately, the current social worker assigned to the branch jail was a kayaking buddy of LP's. He could save LP a lot of time and red tape. LP dug up George Handy's work number and gave him a call.

"Hey, George, can you do me a big favor? You have the run of the jail, and I was hoping you could get the records officer out there to check on a couple guys I have on my caseload. I think both of them were out at the branch about the same time. Both got pretty light sentences, and they might have gotten to be trustees. Could you find out when each went in and out of custody out there? And is there any chance they may have had access to each other while out there? I'd like to know if they were given work projects together or anything like that. I'd also like to know if they knew each other out there, and if so, I'll tell you why later. But try not to get the jailers all suspicious about any big investigation or any big deal. The names are John Richards, receiving stolen property, and Raymond Linn, possession of a sawed-off shotgun."

"Okay, Sherlock Holmes. I'll see what I can do and get back to you later. Have you been out in the boat lately?"

"Once or twice a week when I can sneak out there. If I don't, my boat gets mad at me. Call me when you get the information."

If LP could tie those jailbirds together, it could solve a riddle or two. Otherwise, how did they find each other to make a big drug transaction?

CHAPTER 13

The next morning, LP had Don back with him, and both agreed getting out of the office was a good plan. Before leaving, LP had to do a little paper shuffling.

A few days had passed since LP had submitted his good-bye letter, and everyone in the building knew about the big plan. The building's population wasn't entirely composed of angry, cussing males. On a more positive side, there were a number of female POs on board. Many had worked their way out of juvenile hall. All were good, tough, streetwise people who could handle their jobs as good as or better than most of the men. Before LP and Don got out the door, Shirley Luster, one of the female probation officers, struck up a conversation with LP in the hallway. She congratulated him on his decision to quit.

After they talked briefly about that, she added, "I have a great idea. A few of us are getting together at my place on Saturday evening for a little swim and a few drinks. I have a pool in my backyard. You've never been over for any of our pool parties. One reason for the party is we're trying to cheer up Margorie Woods. You know her. She works for the welfare department. She hangs out with a bunch of us. She just broke up with her boyfriend, and she is really in the dumps. Your presence would help in adding a little cheer. We could celebrate your liberation at the same time. Why don't you be a sport and come on over?"

Without hesitation, LP said, "It sounds great to me. I'll try to dig up a few of my old, stale jokes, and maybe I'll bring my harmonica. No, I better not bring my harmonica. That could get all of us in the dumps."

LP reveled at the thought of a party. It had been a hot summer, and he could always stand a dip in a pool. Besides that, Shirley Luster was a real looker. Every time LP saw her in the hall, he almost drooled. She was a very nice person too.

She added, "Seven o'clock p.m., and it's very informal, but you can't get in without a swimsuit. You don't need to bring anything. I even provide the towels. Just bring those stale jokes. That's what we all need."

This was a first for LP. He'd worked in this office for quite a long stretch, and none of the POs did much socializing together. After work everybody seemed to go in different directions faster than the speed of light. A few played a little golf together or hoisted a few at a neighborhood bar, but LP had cashed his chips in on those adventures in the distant past.

Minutes after the party invitation, LP and Don were out the door and out of the dungeon into the warm, sunny world LP loved. LP decided that a good place to try first would be the man he and Don had seen in the office the previous week. The guy said he was between jobs, so he probably hadn't rolled out of bed this early in the morning—that is, if he was still in town. Besides that, he explained to Don that he had sent a postcard to the man earlier telling him to expect a call from the probation officer today. LP explained that cards were often sent to some of the people on the caseload to let them know when the POs planned to see them. Most of them, however, got no such warnings. If people got cards and couldn't be home on the appointment date, they were instructed to call probation and arrange some other plan.

LP had received no notice from Mr. Motorcycle Man, so he should be around. When they got to their destination, a young lady met them at the front door. She explained that the short-lived new boyfriend had taken off a few days earlier and took all of his belongings with him. She hadn't heard from him since then. LP felt like slapping palms with Don but nodded his head in Don's direction. She didn't know if he had gotten LP's card because she worked all last week and he said nothing about any card.

LP said, "I'm sorry to hear that, but who knows, it might have been a lucky break for you. It definitely isn't a good break for him, though. If he doesn't show up soon, we will issue a warrant for him. If he comes back, tell him to come see me. He knows where the probation office is. What we will do now is send a registered letter to this address for him. Don't sign for it. If it is not signed for, the letter will come back to us, and we have evidence that he has run. The court will issue a warrant for his arrest. He will have made a very bad decision, but it will be his decision."

As they got into the car, LP said, "We hit a bull's-eye on that guy. I hope he shows up like right now. That way we wouldn't have to file on him. I don't know why some people can't do things right. They get a choice, and they end up shooting themselves in the foot. Then they blame everybody else. If he doesn't show up, we have to wait until the letter he doesn't pick up is returned. That's usually a week or longer. After that, we prepare the papers for the court. If I'm gone before we face that, the boss will help you on that or else just ask anybody in the unit. It's pretty simple."

LP said, "I'll tell you what, Don, let's have a little fun while we're doing the job. Kill two birds with one stone. The one we are going to see next doesn't know it, but he is going to be part of the act. I've heard from another probationer there's somebody in this area who's been selling drugs—apparently a lot of drugs. This fellow we are going to see often seems to know what is going on around here. He's lived in this area all of his life. He's dropped me a clue or two in the past, but you have to pry it out of him. He doesn't want to become known as a snitch. Who would?

"Anyway, let's head over there. He's an antique car collector. He has a small collection of old junky cars, mostly inoperable, in a barn next to his house. He's on probation because he was stopped one night driving around half drunk. The police found some electrical stuff, TVs or auto parts most likely, in the trunk. The police found out that the items were stolen property. Although he maintained he had bought the things in good faith, he still got a receiving stolen property conviction along with a drunken driving rap. He had previous drunk driving convictions, so he lost his driver's license also.

"I believe he could be a bit of a fence, but I never see anything lying around that looks out of place. But it's hard to tell because he does have a lot of junk, and I mean junk, lying around in the barn. Most of his cars could be classified as junk if you ask me. He tinkers around on those cars and does some car repair for others. But it doesn't appear he can make a living on that amount of work.

"What I propose to do is to get him to give me a little information to appease me and to keep me off of his back. Indirectly, what I tell him is that I think I saw him driving his car, which is something he can't do on probation. It's a probation violation. I want him to know that I actually did see this happen but that I am giving him a break and plan to forget it. I forget it if he helps me out with a little information. This is probably going to sound like an Abbott and Costello routine, and I hope I don't put my foot in my mouth and blow it.

"Don't laugh, just look grim. Just watch and enjoy. See how the pros do it. We aren't going to do anything illegal. I need a couple of people to give me verification that a crime is being committed hereabouts. One other guy already has mentioned to me that this is happening. If I can get Ollie Wilson to confirm that drugs are coming out of a store on the boulevard, that makes two confirmations. I know of another person who will very likely know about it too. With three people telling me there are drugs flowing out of that store, I will call the cops and suggest some sort of raid."

When they pulled into Ollie Wilson's yard, he was sitting in a chair at the entrance of his barn.

"Ollie, this is your new probation officer, Don Lamond," said LP as they walked over to the barn.

"How come you aren't going to be my probation officer anymore?" asked Ollie.

"Well, Ollie, they're putting me out to pasture because my brain is turning to pudding from you guys giving me the runaround all the time. You'll have to shape up from here on because Mr. Lamond is no pushover like me."

Don walked into the garage and studied the small car collection. All of the vehicles looked neglected except for the one near the barn door. It appeared to be in much better shape than the others. LP and Ollie joined him, and Ollie said, "That's a LaSalle four-door touring Sedan made by General Motors."

LP spoke up. "I know a little about those LaSalle cars. This one is either a 1938 or 1939, V8, with the suicide car doors. Look at these rear doors, Don; they call them suicide doors because the door hinges are to the rear. Apparently they made them that way even though if the door opened when you were speeding down the road, you could fall out and get killed. A lot of cars had that feature back in those days, but not anymore."

LP continued, "You wouldn't believe this, but I had a buddy back in high school whose dad was a mechanic, and he bought a secondhand LaSalle just like this. It was either a thirty-eight or thirty-nine model. My buddy, Paul, begged his dad to let him take it out for a little ride around town. His dad agreed, so Paul picked up a bunch of us, and we went for a spin. We took it outside the town to the highway; a narrow two-lane gravel road. Paul decided to see how fast it would go and floored it down the road. We were skidding around a bit, and it felt like we must have been going about a hundred miles an hour for a minute or two. It was a miracle, but we survived. Later Paul's dad had the LaSalle up on the grease rack in the garage and found a lot of gravel up on the car frame under the car. He asked Paul if he knew anything about that. Well of course Paul had to give his dad a big lie. He said, 'Gosh, Dad, I don't know how that gravel got there. When I drove it, we just drove it up and down Main Street and honked the horn at some of the girls.' Luckily, Paul's dad bought the lie."

Don couldn't take his eyes off of the car and said, "There sure is a lot of car here, and it's a real beauty. Does it run?"

"It runs real good," said Ollie. "I've done a lot of work on it, and I don't think I'll ever sell it."

LP wanted to get to the core of the matter and began, "As rare as this car is, it's not the only LaSalle around here. About a week ago, when I was headed back to the office, I saw a car just like this. I was driving up to the intersection of Elm Street on Morgan Avenue, and just before I got to the intersection, this LaSalle crossed through the intersection in front of me. I couldn't see who was driving it, but it was a LaSalle just like this. I know it wasn't you, Ollie, because you can't drive since they revoked your license. That would be a violation of probation. So somebody else around here has one of these babies too. That's something, isn't it?"

"Yes, it certainly is," replied Ollie. "I'd like to find out who else has one of these. They are very rare, you know. They might have spare parts, too."

"I've never seen one of these before," said Don. "I wonder why they quit making them."

LP answered, "Packard and General Motors were competing in the big car area at that time, and GM decided to put all their effort into Cadillac and to drop the LaSalle. None were made after 1939."

LP hoped his mention of the phantom second LaSalle sunk in with Ollie. He wanted Ollie to get some kind of a message. After a bit, LP brought up the subject of Margareta's murder, commenting that it was very strange.

Ollie responded, "She got along with everybody around here and never bothered anybody that I know of."

LP said, "I guess you knew she did a little work over at the import store. I heard through the grapevine that there was some drug traffic going on over there. Do you suppose there was some connection there?"

After a short pause, Ollie replied, "I had noticed that lately there has been a bit of traffic over there that didn't look like they were souvenir shoppers."

"Are you saying somebody over there is selling dope? Maybe somebody in the store?"

Ollie responded, "Well, you never know. It's just something that I noticed. I could be wrong. But I don't think Margareta was sharp enough to be running any drug operation."

LP looked at his watch and said, "Uh oh. I'd like to hang around a little longer and talk about cars, but we have to get going. Good luck to you, and don't give Don any grief, okay?"

After they drove off, LP said, "You heard what he said. I take it that he is agreeing there must be some mischief going on over there. That means we have confirmation number two. And I hope to have number three very soon. Speaking of my pal Paul and his big lie, what did you think about the one I spun back there?"

Don looked confused and said, "Which one was that?"

"The whole thing about the LaSalle. The other day I went to the library to get some information on the LaSalle to get into it with Ollie."

Don looked confused and asked, "What about the one you drove around in in high school?"

"Oh, I made that up too. Pretty good, huh? I did have a pal named Paul, though, and his dad did have a LaSalle."

"What about the one you drove in high school?"

"Oh, I made that up too. It sounded real, didn't it? Paul's dad didn't let us take it out and drive it at a hundred miles an hour. I just added that for a little color."

At that, LP and Don chuckled for a few minutes.

"Talking about lies today, I have come to believe everybody lies at one time or another. I even lie. You witnessed that today. It's the first line of defense in self-preservation. Lie, lie, lie. I was thinking about all the lies you will get out here.

"I wonder how many times I've heard a mother of a juvenile probationer say something like this, 'My son might steal a car or he might burglarize a neighbor or skip school for weeks, but he would never lie to me.' It just makes me want to double up laughing at them. Junior lies to Mom, and Mom lays a tall one on you."

LP decided he might as well hog the soapbox a little more and continued. "Speaking of juveniles, you will have about twenty-five or thirty juveniles in your caseload and about seventy or seventy-five adults. You will spend two-thirds of your time with the juveniles. One of the POs in the unit refused to supervise any juveniles, and they don't give him any. I won't tell you which PO it is, but he is the grouchiest one in the unit. The others are just normal grouchy. He is a good PO, though. They may be afraid he might quit if he had to chase around after a bunch of kids.

"Many of the kids will drive you crazy. The biggest problem with them is their parents. You are dealing with the parents as much as with the juveniles. In many cases, the parent is partly the cause of the kid getting on probation. They are either too strict or too lax. The kids manipulate the parent or the parent tries to control the kid too much.

"When I was working in juvenile court, I got a case of a kid who was going to court over a car theft, and I was preparing the report for the court. The juvenile and his friends were stealing cars and stripping them for parts to sell. The group was using several of the parental garages to do their work. This family lived in a semirural, low-income part of the city. In this part of the city, you could see old abandoned cars, refrigerators, stoves, and junk in many of the front yards and a few goats grazing in the weeds. Not any college professors living around there, I would think.

"When I arrived, I talked briefly to the mother in the family kitchen. Very shortly her son came into the kitchen, and before any introduction, he remarked to mom, 'Ma, why don't you get us some Popeye's chicken for lunch?' Her son was a big, muscular, blond-haired sixteen-year-old. But the most notable thing about him was a large brass belt buckle on his pants. Inscribed on the belt buckle, in large letters, were the words, 'LET'S F**K,' and all of the letters were in their proper place. The letters were large enough that any person could read them from twenty feet away. Apparently Mom had no objection to Junior walking around with his belt like that. At the time I had to hold back the urge to advise the kid to be sure to wear that belt to court for the judge to enjoy. Perhaps he did without my great suggestion.

"I could only wonder what he hoped to achieve by wearing something like that. He had to be a bit thick between the ears. However, if you are going to choose to be a car thief to make a living, it really isn't important what impression you make on people around you. It appeared that anything Junior did was okay with Mom. Let the young man fully explore who he is. If he was job hunting while wearing his prized belt buckle, do you think prospective employers would be fighting each other to sign him up? Not likely.

"That was a sample of a very compromising parent. There are parents who raise their children from a different perspective that is equally questionable. On the other hand, I had a bright young boy who hated his father and did all he could to antagonize the parent. The father treated the son the same way. The parent was a very conservative and domineering preacher who wanted total control over the son's activities. In one area, the son didn't want to attend church services, but the father insisted that the boy sit through all services. There was conflict in every other area of life also. To counter the parents' rules, the son was skipping school and doing about everything within the law to upset his dad, and it did. As the PO, it was very defeating to endlessly listen to them quarreling and watching them getting into each other's faces. They could agree on nothing. The first thing the PO had to remember was to not take sides, and the mention of counseling went right over their heads. At one point the son found out from somewhere that his father wasn't his real father. He was his stepfather. From there, things worsened. If people don't seek counseling and their attitudes don't change, there is never any common ground.

"And there is always a group of parents that can't handle their children. They will call the PO and demand that you come and take the child away. They want us to put him in juvenile hall and don't bring him back, even though he has committed no crime."

LP hoped some of his marathon orations were of some worth to Don. It appeared that by now he was getting fully saturated with a lot of useless information. Don had worked with and supervised juveniles in juvenile hall and was prepared for any surprises that would come at him shortly. Juveniles behave differently when they aren't in custody, however. LP wanted to alert Don to what he might run into on the new job. It might be helpful.

CHAPTER 14

Finally it was Friday, and Don was back in the hall for the day. LP hoped he could coast into the weekend. It had been an eventful week, and a lot had to be done before he finally closed the books. He kept thinking of the Saturday-evening invitation to the swim party at Shirley's. If he had time, he had to run out and buy a new swimsuit. All he had were a bunch of worn-out, faded ones. He didn't want to show up looking like a tramp.

Before he finished his second cup of coffee, LP decided to call Sheriff's Officer Hal Schaefer who had earlier requested information on the Raymond Linn place.

Fortunately, Schaefer was available and informed LP, "The court gave us a warrant, and we did make the search. You mentioned the gated front porch, and we had to use a wrecker and chain to pull that door open. We found a large amount of narcotics in his place as well as firearms. Linn is now in the county jail awaiting his arraignment. There is no way he can beat this rap. He is headed for prison."

LP said, "Good. No more breaks for him. He will also get a violation of probation charge added to any conviction.

Somebody might get a good price on a relatively new Chevy Corvette. Of course, that will depend on his lawyer. He will probably get it first. If not him, then one of Linn's criminal cronies. Thanks for the information."

After the call, LP felt like he was on a roll. He decided to call his pal George Handy at the branch jail. Maybe he could make it two in a row.

This was beginning to be a good day for crime fighters. LP got George on the second ring. "George, what are you doing? It appears that you just sit at a desk with your telephone. When do you go out among your flock and hold their hands while they are breaking up huge boulders with sledgehammers?"

"Very funny, very funny. Listen, if you don't treat me with large amounts of respect, I may not let you know what I found out about your two pals, Mr. John Richards and Mr. Raymond Linn."

"Oh, forgive me, honorable social worker and healer. I'll have my tongue removed at the first opportunity. Okay, give me the dope on those two rascals. I need a little positive news once in a while to keep me going. It's been slim pickings lately, and I think Slim just left the room."

"Well the news appears to be interesting. Both Richards and Linn were in the branch jail during the same period. Both were allowed to do trustee work, and would you believe it, they both worked in the kitchen, so there was no way they didn't cross paths out here at the branch. And listen to this: all trustees are housed together in a large living and sleeping area, just like an army barracks. I'm sure you've seen an army barracks or two in your colored past. Your guys could sit around and cook up all kinds of crooked adventures together. By the time they got out of there, they must have been the best of friends. What do you need this information for? It sounds like you are making like Dick Tracy, cracking another big case for law and order."

"Well you might be close there. Raymond Linn just got picked up on a big drug possession bust. Lots and lots of drugs and some guns, I guess. Without a doubt he is headed for the big house this time. No county jail time for him this time. Don Lamond and I heard through the grapevine that Richards might be getting into the business as a peddler, big time too. There's nothing concrete on that, but where there is smoke there may be fire, and I don't mean cigar smoke. But listen, don't spread anything around because this is just guesswork for now. I wouldn't want you to get your foot stuck in your mouth on my account. Just wait for my next communique."

George asked, "Who is Don Lamond? Have you got a new boss?"

LP responded, "I guess I forgot to tell you. I'm quitting my job at the end of this month. I'm counting the hours. Don is going to be my replacement. After the end of the month, they will have a real probation officer in place of me."

"What the heck are you going to do if you quit your job? You'll starve to death. You'll never find a good job like the one you have been abusing for years. I'll guarantee you will regret it after the first week. You must have lost your mind."

"Well, this work routine is cramping my kayaking time too much, and if I quit, I can go out in the boats all day long. You can't row a boat in the dark, you know. I thought I might look around for a night watchman's job and I'll have all kinds of time to get some fun out of the daylight. Don't worry, I'll be around. I'll see you later, and thanks for this good information. While I'm gone, take care of your little chums out at the branch jail."

At this point, LP decided he had to sit down and sort out all these little bits and pieces of information that had been dribbling in. He wasn't going to do that until he saw a couple people today. These contacts could be fruitful.

As for sorting things out, the best place LP knew of to get away from it all and do some heavy thinking was on the river. Saturday morning would be reserved for that. An hour on the river would be perfect. He could just sop it up, take it easy, and save a little strength for the upcoming Saturday-evening party. And while drifting along, he could get a little more of a tan on the old bones.

His first stop would be to see Margareta's roommate downtown. He had only seen the roommate for a few minutes on the day he verified Margareta's change of address. The roommate was a rather meek-acting guy. He didn't enter into their conversation on the day LP confirmed Margareta lived there. He just scurried around straightening up things in the kitchen and living room, as if he was the only one in the apartment.

He had forgotten the roommate's name even though he had recorded it in his field book at the time of the previous visit, but all of that information was now drawing dust in closed files. When he got to the entrance of the apartment complex, he checked the mailboxes for the name of Mr. Roommate. He hoped Donald Darey would be around and full of information today. Fortunately, he was home when LP rapped on his door.

"Hello, I don't know if you remember who I am. I was Margareta's probation officer, and I wonder if you could give me just a couple of minutes. It might shed some light on who killed Margareta. From what I know about Margareta, she certainly didn't deserve what happened to her."

"I'll tell you the little I know about Margareta if you think it will help you out."

"One thing I was wondering about was did the police come to see you for information that would help them?"

"No, they didn't. But I don't think they even knew Margareta was staying here. She just moved in after she did her jail time."

"It sounds like when she got bumped off, it was just a part of the skid row routine," responded LP. "There wasn't much to go on, I guess, and now she's gone and pretty much forgotten. After that brief article in the newspaper about the killing, I kept looking for more details, but there was never anything after that. Tell me, did she ever mention her job to you?"

"Oh yes, she did. Margareta was happy to have that work even though it hardly paid anything. A couple of days before she disappeared, she was very pleased because her boss was going to give her a raise and some added responsibilities at the job. I don't know what the new job was, but Margareta was looking forward to it."

"Have you ever been out to where she worked?" asked LP.

"No. I was never invited."

"I've never been in there either. I guess I better take a peek at the place sometime soon. It doesn't sound like Margareta had a lot of money. What about her money situation?"

Donald replied, "Margareta probably had every penny of hers in her purse, and I would imagine most of that was pennies. She had to shell out a lot for bus fare too. She didn't have a car, you know? Would you like a cup of coffee? I have some warm coffee on the stove."

"That sounds like a winner to me. I was thinking Margareta's death had something to do with drugs. Do you know if Margareta used drugs?"

"Definitely not. She didn't drink that much either."

"Do you think Margareta was selling drugs to help support herself?"

Donald shook his head. "No. If that was the case, she would have had some money. She was usually broke when she was around here."

"Did you know if she had any enemies?"

"None that I know of."

"Well, Donald, I want to thank you for your time, and I might nudge the police with the information you gave me. But don't worry about them. It appears law enforcement has bigger fish to fry and has assessed the matter as a quarrel among the unfortunates down along the river."

LP knew the statement he had just said made little sense. Why would a downtown drunk or wino kill Margareta and then drag her body ten miles upriver and throw her body into the river up there? The river was just a few blocks from skid row downtown. That certainly made no sense. But more accurately, it might make sense that the person who killed Margareta had to have a car or truck, and they didn't want her body to be found.

They wanted that body to be washed out to sea. No wino would go through all that trouble.

"I had one other question, Donald," said LP. "Do you know if Margareta had any friends living up near where her body was found?"

"She never went out that way as long as I knew her."

As he left, LP thanked the roommate and added that the information he gave was very helpful.

LP was glad he was able to talk to the roommate. It showed a pattern of what could have gone down. Now he would go see someone who might share a bit more information on the matter. This person would be available for certain because he was snug as a bug in the county jail and wasn't going anywhere for a long time.

He would have no problem seeing Raymond Linn unless he was in court today. LP had his shiny PO badge that could get him into the jail almost any time. Field officers rarely had to go into the jail to see anyone. Court officers were in and out daily, getting information from criminals to complete their court reports. These reports had a heavy bearing on the fate of the convicted person. If asked by the jailers, why he was seeing Raymond Linn, LP could say it related to the violation of probation papers he was organizing for the likely conviction on the new arrest.

It was very convenient that POs, lawyers, and others involved in these cases could see the defendant in a special area of the jail that had privacy as opposed to the visitor's area. And when you requested to see the person, the jailers got him in front of you without delay.

LP had no problem getting what he asked for. After going through numerous locked doors and up a few floors to the visitor's area, he got a seat at a desk where he would be able to talk to Mr. Linn. When Linn showed up, he reacted like he didn't know who LP was. That's normal when you've only crossed paths once or twice. Linn likely thought, *I don't know this guy. What good is he going to do me?*

LP reintroduced himself. "Do you remember me? I'm your probation officer. I think we only got together about one time, and here you are, back in the can. You are a fast worker. My name is LP Cinch; I gave you my card when I saw you over at your place. It sounds like this is serious business this time."

LP continued, "If you get convicted of a new offense, probation will file a violation because of that. That way if you are sentenced for something, the violation of probation will be handled in court at the same time. Does that make sense? Just a little more paperwork. It would be a big stretch if you got any more probation. Probably zero."

LP gave the man a touch of false hope. It would be beyond a miracle.

Linn said, "I don't want any more probation. I'll just do my time."

LP figured he'd get that response. Spoken like a true son. He had heard that more than once over the years. Now LP hoped he could get something else from him—just nudge him a bit.

"Do you remember Margareta?"

Looking puzzled, Linn said, "Margareta? Who's that?"

LP let him dwell on that momentarily and then put a small smile on his face and said, "The ugly guy who goes around in an ugly dress and sells you a big bag of dope. Over on the boulevard, remember?"

Linn gazed at LP and said nothing.

LP came back with more. "She got bumped off. Shot in the back of the head and dumped in the river."

Linn didn't move a muscle. Not a peep.

"I guess he tried to waltz off with the dough but Richards caught up with him and paid him off with a bullet. I'm sure you remember Richards; he's the guy you know from the county jail. Remember?"

After pondering that briefly, Linn said, "That name sounds vaguely familiar, but I can't seem to place it." He appeared to break into a subtle grin that matched LP's earlier grin.

LP decided he had just gotten a positive response.

To keep the conversation going in the right direction, LP went on. "Well, who has the dough? Richards probably. He probably squeezed it out of Margareta and then just shot him for fun. A good way to cut down on witnesses, right?

"There was no way that you didn't know Margareta worked for Richards. I just wanted you to know what kind of friend he was. He just used Margareta to do his dirty work and keep his risk of exposure to a minimum. Nice guy, huh?"

"It sounds like a very tragic story, but as I said before, I don't recall meeting any Richards."

"Come on, Linn, give me a break. Let me refresh your memory. You and Richards worked side by side in the branch jail kitchen while you were both out there. You both were housed in the trustee barracks. You sat around every evening out there, nose to nose, cooking up your master drug deal. Do I look like a big dummy? Don't answer that. Anyway, it would be nice to see Richards get a little of what he handed out to others. But you're out of this end of the deal, so don't sweat it.

"These violation of probation papers won't be an issue until after a conviction," said LP. "Don't even think about them. If you have a court trial, you will be sitting here for longer than a month. My guess is that bail is almost impossible; a big, big stretch. You may not see me again. It's a shame you won't get to cruise around in that Corvette for a while."

"Yes, you may be right, but I got a pretty good lawyer. We'll see how it goes."

"Watch out. These lawyers are pretty slick. I may be seeing him driving that Corvette around the city in a couple months with you not aboard."

LP left him with that bit of wisdom. His instincts told him that Linn hadn't come anywhere near close to saying Richards wasn't the man. It sounded like Richards was elected as the big dude. LP wasn't certain how Linn would handle this conversation. Linn might get word back to Richards that LP was hot on his trail. He hoped that wasn't the case. In that case, he should call the law enforcement and fill them in as soon as possible. He hoped that wouldn't happen because he wanted to make one final contact before he gave the police an important call.

On his way home, LP decided to see what the postman had left him in the PO box he had rented earlier. When he peeked into the tiny window on the box, he was surprised to see a few envelopes. *My, my. It looks like I have a few fans who lost some money or just wanted a little green for themselves.* In the box were six letters and one postcard. LP grabbed them and planned to read what he got as soon as he got home.

At home, after his review of the correspondence, he could see that these respondents were trying to avoid details and hoped LP would accept their vague stories. Some said the money was in a plain envelope and the exact amount was unknown since some of the cash had been spent earlier. All claimed their loss occurred in the same zip code area as the post office branch. A couple said the money was in a wad that dropped out of a pocket and had a total value of about two or three hundred dollars.

One writer tried the sympathy approach. LP got an extended message detailing unemployment, rent due, and hungry children. This one volunteered to give LP half of the money as a reward if he would send the balance to the starving man. LP had to give him first place among all the failed approaches. This was another case of close but no cigar.

LP bundled all the letters together and saved them for evidence that he had made a major effort to return the lost wealth to the true owner. There might be more letters to come.

By now it was Friday evening. He had to decide what to do with this house, which he owned. He didn't want to sell it now and possibly not later. A bigger issue was the household's contents. There were a few valuables in the house that he didn't want stolen or destroyed. They would be a great find for thieves and would be a great loss to LP. The best place for a few of these things would be storage in a rental locker. He could simply dump those things there for a brief time, even a month or less.

By then he should have figured out the course of things to come. His big trip could have fizzled out very quickly. His roots were very deep in Two Rivers. It would be difficult to leave his haunts behind. One positive thing was that he could go on recess for now and not saddle himself with any long-term commitments to anyone, including himself. He could just let the big plans come later.

CHAPTER 15

L P never had a hard time getting up in the morning when he had a day off. Today was especially good. It was a very warm 6:00 a.m. when he began to load his boat and bike on to the car. LP, his kayak, and his thirty-year-old Schwinn, one-speed bike were as happy as clams. The river was LP's favorite think tank. There was one important job to do before the trip started. LP had to scramble around and get Margareta's money out of its safe hiding place. He would leave that behind today. If the boat ever flipped on him, he would end up with a lot of wet money. He could see the money drifting softly away from him downriver as he tried to upend his kayak. That could arouse a little attention for certain. It was a rare event when LP flipped in the river unintentionally, but it had happened a few interesting times in the past.

This hour in the river would give him much time alone to put some of the puzzle together regarding the murder and the money. At a little after 6:00 a.m., his counseling couch awaited him. The only spectators were a few birds and fish.

LP decided to go from A to Z on the events that had occurred. First of all, John Richards and Ray Linn had set up and arranged for a drug transaction in jail months ago. Richards was the man who got the dope into the country. How he did it was unknown, but very likely he was able to get the drugs in his hands through shipments of legal goods from Asia. It may have taken a number of shipments to achieve what he needed. Or he could have brought drugs into the country himself. His job assignments included trips to the Orient as part of his job as a civilian air force engine specialist. LP wasn't certain how he could pull that off, but he didn't think military aircraft had to go through any customs searches. Richards must have built up a large supply and met with Linn in jail. Linn could have been connected with one of the motorcycle gangs that were heavily into the drug business. Whoever was going to buy the stuff had to have a super-large wallet to make a buy like that.

Linn and Richards got together after their jail time and arranged to do the deal. Richards didn't want to expose himself to any risk he could avoid, so he used Margareta as a mule. Richards didn't want the transaction to occur in his store as a further precaution, so he saddled Margareta up with the goods and sent her out to complete the sale. Linn and Margareta met in the parking lot of the dumpy bowling alley on the boulevard. They made the switch and headed out in different directions. However, as Margareta strolled on the dusty path at the side of the road back to the store, things began to go wrong. The last people Margareta wanted to see were the cops coming her way. It must have been a quiet evening for the police because they picked Margareta up for some unknown reason, probably just to give her a hard time. In any event, after that, the rest is history. LP's little group of three and dog, being good Samaritans, sealed Margareta's fate: a death sentence.

When Margareta came back early the next morning, probably before sunup, she couldn't find her purse anywhere. She had no idea it was laying under Earle Swope's bed. She knew one thing: she was in deep, deep trouble. The only thing she could do was hide out from her boss. It didn't take Richards long to run her down. Somehow he must have coaxed her back to the store.

When Margareta tried to explain what happened, Mr. Murderer bought none of it. She had the money, and one way or another, he was going to get it out of her. From the appearance of her body, it was evident Richards had used cigarette burns to get Margareta to come clean. Margareta couldn't, though; the money was gone. It had disappeared, like it or not. As time passed, Richards got a little bit more than irked with his employee, and off to the river they went.

LP finally came up with a theory as to why the body had ended up over ten miles from her haunts and the boulevard. LP could make a case that the killer, Richards, had a good-sized cargo vehicle, a requirement for a store owner with goods going in and out of the store daily. And it just so happened that the place where Margareta was dumped was just under two miles from where the murderer worked—the local military air force base. It would be quite simple for the murderer to use this place, which he was quite familiar with. The dumping job occurred at night after dark when no one was around. The bike trails and river entrances were closed daily after dark. Although no one was allowed in these areas after dark, that didn't present a problem. There was one easy resolution. All Richards had to do was get a map of the city and see that at one point a city street along the levee came within fifteen feet of the bike trail and the river. And to make the access absolutely simple, there was a very small parking lot where the road converged with the trail. All the killer had to do was lead the victim or drag his body out of the small lot to the paved bike trail and to the nearby riverbank. Simple as that. LP planned to look at the area today on his return bike ride to his car.

It seemed that LP had all the answers except for two—the two most important ones. How could LP direct things so

Richards got what he had coming? And of course, what should he do with that bag full of the stuff dreams are made of?

As LP glided through the crystal-clear, cool water deep in thought, his eyes focused downriver about one hundred yards. The ducks were also up early today. Flying upriver toward LP were four adult mallards at about fifteen feet above the water. They showed no fear of this laboring paddler. They flew directly over LP's head and continued onward upriver. Something like this was always a bonus for rolling out of bed before sunup. LP's problem was that he hardly ever took a camera along. When he did, the birds usually took that day off.

Further downriver, LP came to shore where Margareta had met her maker. From the bike trail, the parking lot was barely visible but easily accessible. After examining that area, LP was certain the killer had used that parking lot to get to the place of the crime.

This day in the river would be the last for LP for a while. As he returned, home he stopped at a rental storage place near his home and initiated a rental. He was the owner of his residence, and he could return to it later or sell it. His home and possessions would be safe in his absence. However, he had items he wished to keep very safe. He had two kayaks. One would go in to storage. He would also store his faithful, ancient Schwinn bike, worthless as it was. Of major concern was his fairly sizable collection of coins. Over the years, LP had remained a collector of silver and gold US and foreign coins. After years of fast food joints and TV dinners, the undirected collection of coins piled up, the reason unknown. It would be something burglars would find very rewarding.

In addition to that, he had a sizable collection of big band and jazz LPs and CDs, a second bad habit. The days of good jazz and the long-playing albums with their beautiful album covers had seen their better days and were becoming part of the past. LP couldn't part with these jewels. He would feel more secure with this bulky collection safely in the locker.

He also had a few pieces of collectable art on his walls. They would also take the trip to the darkened, secure locker.

By the time he finished his labor, it was time to prepare for an evening of relaxation with friends. The evening would be warm, and a dip in the pool was just what the doctor ordered.

CHAPTER 16

"**O**h rats," LP uttered to himself. "I forgot to buy a new suit today for the swim this evening."

He would have to dig through his pile of aging, faded swimsuits he used on the river. He would be wearing his swimsuit under his trousers and might not even get close to the water, so he decided to use what he had available. He hoped he had picked the least ugly item to wear. There wasn't much choice.

By the time LP completed his homework for the day, the sun was beginning to sink in the west. As he drove to the party, he hoped a lot of people from work would show up. That way he could kick back and get lost in the crowd. He perceived himself as a listener as opposed to a toastmaster. Knowing who would probably show up, he assessed that the group would focus on drinking, and LP did enjoy, in a way, observing boozers at play. After all, that was partly why he had spent his past life sitting around in bars. The drunks kept the conversation rolling and wanted to blab everything that crossed their minds. He had been there and done that.

As LP drove up the street to Shirley's house, he noticed there were only two cars parked in front of the place. He had expected he would have a hard time finding a parking place. He lucked out tonight. He must be getting there a little early. Better to show up early and leave early.

As he exited his car, he heard laughing and music coming from Shirley's backyard. He decided to go through the backyard gate to the noisy group.

To his surprise, there were only three bikini-clad babes in the large, grass-covered yard: Shirley Luster, her sidekick from work, Ginger Powell, and the jilted social worker, Marjorie Woods. All were relaxing in lounge chairs near the pool. It was fully apparent that the drinking had already begun. Everybody was super-relaxed.

The large backyard was well maintained and surrounded by a seven-foot, vine covered fence. The pool was fairly small but adequate for the size of the yard. The water was blue and inviting. Shrubs and flowers were here and there. As LP closed in on the ladies, he asked, "Where is everybody? Am I here too early?"

Shirley had a big smile on her face and said, "For now, I guess we are everybody. We asked a few others to come, and they may show up soon. But maybe they forgot about us. That's okay; three's company, and four is a crowd."

The girls all giggled at the pun. They didn't seem distressed about the no-shows.

"Grab a drink, and pull up a chair," said Marjorie. "It's time to celebrate."

On a table nearby were numerous bottles of booze, ice, chips, and other snacks. LP walked over and filled a paper cup with 7UP and ice and grabbed a handful of potato chips.

As he sat down in one of the lawn chairs, Shirley asked, "What's with the soda, LP? Are you on the wagon or something? You're not a teetotaler, are you?"

"I've got nothing against drinking, long live Jim Beam, but I hung up my serape a long time ago," said LP. "At one time I was a world-renowned boozer. I used to know every bartender in town. My ex and I used to practically live in a bar. We supported a lot of bartenders in this town. You might say I was a light drinker. I started drinking as soon as it got light."

Shirley said, "Oh, LP, I didn't know you were married."

"Yes, I was a wedded man. A married, drinking man. Finally one morning I told my old lady that I was going on the wagon for a while. I think I had one hangover too many. I just got tired of it. It didn't make sense anymore. I needed to take a little recess.

"The dear wife said she had no plan like that for her. She added, 'I think I have a few drinks I haven't drunk yet. You're spoiling the fun. It's business as usual for me. Be a party pooper if you want. Join the party or stay home.'"

LP continued, "She partied, and I stayed home. After a couple months of that, she made a big announcement. She said, 'I'm splitting for Las Vegas where things are livelier. It's too big a drag here. Are you coming along?'

"'Absolutely not. That's crazy.'

"So she took off without me. I thought she would fit in real good down there where the saloons are open twenty-four hours a day, three hundred sixty-five days a year. She had past jobs and experience in cocktail and restaurant waitressing. There were plenty of those jobs in Vegas. She'd have no trouble finding work or mischief.

"Things seemed to work out for her down there. Shortly after she left, she called and asked me to lend her a few bucks to help with her rent. A couple months after that, she wrote me and said she was in the process of a divorce and would send papers soon. Apparently she met the right sugar daddy or barfly, likely a bartender, to keep company with her. I got some final papers a little later. That chapter of my life was over. I didn't miss her, and I haven't missed the booze. I don't wake up every morning with a splitting headache and an empty wallet. One thing I noticed was that my wallet started putting on weight."

The girls had listened intently and seemed entertained. Maybe, thought LP, his long sermon explained why he was sitting with a 7UP in his hand instead of something more potent. Even so, he had done what he didn't want to do. He had come in and started blabbing his stale life story when it was supposed to be the other way around. He was supposed to listen while the drinkers told it all. Some people just can't get it right, and LP was proof of that.

Shirley had made a good selection of music for the evening. They were listening to the old stuff LP liked, with a lot of big band jazz and some good vocals. The girls continued to hoist the drinks and kept chattering away while LP listened and relaxed. He sipped his soda and enjoyed the view of the three beauties garbed in their bikinis. Ah, what a life.

Finally Ginger said, "Listen, LP, this is a swimming party. Where's your swimsuit? You're breaking the rules."

LP responded, "I've got a swimsuit on. It's just under my pants."

"Well, come on, let's see the great LP in a swimsuit." The other two chimed in and began bugging LP to ditch the Levis.

LP stood up and said, "Okay, okay, I don't want to be a prude. I can see I'm outnumbered here."

As he finished removing his pants, Marjorie piped up in a slightly slurred voice with, "And take off that T-shirt, too. You don't see us wearing any T-shirts, do you? Join the club."

LP smiled at her and complied. Now he was down to his ugly, ugly swimsuit for all to see. He said, "All my tailored suits are at the cleaners."

They all laughed. With the booze, it seemed everything made them laugh. Even the despondent Marjorie was happy as a lark. LP thought to himself, *Now that they've seen my sorry trunks, maybe I will get a chance to try the pool.* That was one of the main reasons why he had come.

They all chatted away and listened to the good music. Finally Shirley got up and said, "Come on LP, let's dance. We can't waste this good music." It was one of Artie Shaw's classics. "You're the only guy here tonight, so you got to do part of the dancing."

LP couldn't think of a reasonable excuse, so the dance began. As the stumbling dance steps continued, LP was hit with a strange, sinister impulse, something he couldn't now or later explain even to himself. Shirley's two-piece top tied at her back. In an instant of juvenile chicanery, he pulled one of the dangling bikini strings. The flimsy garment fell away from the appointed position. Shirley looked down and let out a big loud, "Oh." Immediately her hands came out in front of her, and she gave LP a brisk push on the chest. LP had his back to the edge of the pool. He couldn't step back to avoid her thrust. He could feel that he was totally losing his balance. Then he realized he was about to end up on his back in the pool. As he lost all control of balance, he grabbed Shirley's wrist, hoping she would stop his fall. It didn't help. LP hit the water, and Shirley tumbled into the water with him. Their audience had been closely watching their fabulous dance steps. As they performed their Laurel and Hardy routine, they broke into hysterics. They loved it.

As they bobbed in the water, LP looked at Shirley, whose bikini top was drifting near her in the water. Seeing that Ginny removed her bikini top and threw it in the air, Marjorie followed suit and both laughed with drunken, uncontrolled glee.

Attempting to say something that could perhaps get him off the hook, he said, "Well, Laurel, this is another fine mess you've gotten me into." Their audience roared on, and even Shirley began to laugh. Maybe he would escape with his life after all. He even began to chuckle a bit. It was rather funny and unrehearsed.

In an attempt to mend his ways, LP said, "I think the devil made me do it. But it was kind of fun. Why don't we do this more often?" The audience laughed and hooped in approval.

LP thought a good move was to get out of the pool as gracefully and quickly as possible to just fade away in the night. He began to exit at the pool ladder. At that point, Shirley reached up from the water and grabbed the back of LP's swimsuit. He thought he heard the sound of ripping fabric. As Shirley hung on, LP could feel his suit skidding below his knees. He couldn't move his feet to climb the steps with the tangled trunks at his ankles. Shirley didn't release her hold. At this point, LP was naked as a blue jay in full view of all the peering eyes.

After much effort, he was able to free one foot from captivity and climb to the grass bank but minus his suit. In the pool, Shirley was whirling the prized suit around and around over her head for everyone to see. She released it, and it came to rest on the grass. Everyone except LP continued to crack up with glee.

As he stood before the girls at the edge of the pool, he noted that every eye, except his, was fully focused on him. It's funny how some of the smallest things in life can draw so much attention. LP decided he had to make the best of it. Crying wasn't the course to take tonight. He had to think of something better. A Clark Kent exit from the telephone booth would never do. It had to be a Superman exit.

He stood there for a moment looking down at himself and then extended his arms up in the air and proclaimed in a loud, official voice, "I think the emperor is wearing no clothes." This invoked more laughter. LP took a deep bow in front of Marjorie and Ginger and then turned back to Shirley and gave her a gracious and gentlemanly bow.

At that point, he turned and began to walk to his limp, wet suit lying in the grass. The girls began whistling, and one yelled, "Encore, encore." The other shouted, "Play it again, Sam." LP picked up his suit, made a 360-degree turn, and started pulling up the battered rag.

Marjorie yelled, "Don't put that on yet. It's my turn to dance with you." Then Ginger chimed in, "Curtain call, curtain call."

LP resisted their demands and pulled up his shorts. By now Shirley had exited the pool with her bikini top in hand. Seeing LP putting on his suit, she replaced her top. The others, seeing what was happening, retrieved their tops and put them on too. It looked like the big fun was over for tonight. What started out to be a quiet evening of conversation turned out to be anything but that. When things got out of hand, it became a memorable evening for all. And it was getting late. They had all survived without any cuts, bruises, or bumps on the head. They were now just very good friends who had shared an eventful evening together. But it was time to call it a day. As the old saying goes, close but no cigar.

As LP began to depart, he said to Shirley, "I can give both of your pals a ride home. I don't think they should be doing any driving tonight in their shape." Marjorie appeared to be nodding off.

Shirley said, "That would be a very good idea, but I think I'll just keep them here for the night. Tomorrow is Sunday and no work. Let them sleep it off. They probably won't even remember what happened here tonight. And if they do, we can rehash it over again over breakfast. I hope you enjoyed yourself."

"Well, I have to say I really did have fun. I'm glad you have such a wonderful sense of humor, and from my angle the scenery was . . . let's just say *wow!*"

To the other two, LP said, "Thanks, ladies. Let's have this as our very, very special secret. We won't tell a soul. We'll just keep it in our hearts and not share with anyone."

To Shirley he added, "Don't let them have their car keys, and we can all save some money and extra headaches."

CHAPTER 17

The next morning over a warm cup of coffee, LP reviewed in his mind the antics of the night before. He had no hangover or headache, but he knew of a few people who might be suffering a little. Oh, thank God for sobriety. As far as his behavior last night, he wondered if that was the end of a budding friendship. He hoped not. He had to admit that if the girls wanted to have a little spontaneous entertainment last night, he certainly did his part. He'd have to wait until Monday morning to see if all of the party people had survived and if he was on speaking terms with them. He hoped he wouldn't be banished.

Today he needed to get a little exercise for a change and decided to get his bike out of storage and take a leisurely cruise around the neighborhood. It would give him the opportunity to deal with a growing tug-of-war that was going on in his head over the sack of money.

After rescuing his bike, he began to loosen up with a leisurely ride on the city streets. He was fairly close to the boulevard, and he decided to head over to Richards' gift store.

He could kill two birds with one stone. He had never been in the place. It might be interesting to give it a look.

As he moved along, he decided the money wasn't going to go away, and he wasn't going to abandon it or give it up without a good reason. He had to make a decision that made sense to him.

First of all, he couldn't turn it over to the authorities now. He'd already spent part of it. The authorities had no idea of the existence of any money. There was no crime reported that involved any money. To them, no money existed to investigate. Why give it to them? If you find a dollar in the street, do you call the police and tell them? What about ten dollars? One hundred dollars? One thousand dollars? If the money was sizable, the police would hold it for a period of time, and if no one claimed it, the money would be returned to the finder. As they say, "Finders keepers, losers weepers." What if fifty thousand dollars was surrendered to them? Would they return it to the finder without a never-ending investigation? I doubt it. That money would never see the light of day again. They would dig up some justification for keeping it.

And of course, LP wasn't certain the money had any connection to Margareta's murder. It was just based on hunches and tales of residents of the neighborhood. If the money belonged to Margareta, maybe it was the result of some lawful transaction. No one knew. The actual finders, LP's three chums and their dog, rejected the money. They wanted no part of it. They saddled him with it.

LP had gone through the formality of attempting to locate the owner of the money via the newspaper ads. No results there.

If in fact Richards was the owner of the money through some business transaction, perhaps drugs, he had taken no action to claim it. If that happened, he would risk being exposed as his employee's murderer, and he certainly wouldn't want to tread in those waters.

LP assumed that somewhere in the legal codes there was a law that would require that money involved in a crime had to be surrendered to authorities. But no crime was being investigated.

No crime was reported. Margareta's death was a closed case. And money—what money?

LP researched the penal code for codes explaining the finding of money. Code 1407 PC relates to disposal of property stolen or embezzled, but in this case there was no report that money was stolen or embezzled. There was no report, period.

Laws are laws and rules are rules. But the morality of these can often be adjusted to favor, overlook, or forgive one side or the other. Cheaters at times are not considered cheaters. Morality—what morality? It must depend on who has to do the clarifying. LP could think of a classic situation in which most persons would give their blessings to an act of theft.

In World War II, and probably in many, many other similar situations, sets of theft occurred and no one objected. In this example, the United States used code breakers to listen to the enemy sending coded messages to troops with instructions and plans. The code breakers were able to decode the messages and take advantage of the enemy. That information was stolen. No one objected. Thank goodness for a little cheating.

In baseball games, if one team can steal the signals sent from the opponent's catcher to the pitcher, is that theft? Is it wrong? Is it a criminal offense? Under what penal code does that one fall?

LP felt that his subconscious was saying, *Keep the money.* But the little angel on his left shoulder kept saying, *No, no. Don't do that. Return the money to the owner.* But who was the owner? LP had no intention of giving Mr. Richards one dime. The devil on LP's right shoulder agreed. He kept saying, *It's nobody's money. Just stick it in your pocket and don't make a big deal of it.*

And then LP made a statement to himself. He said, *Take the money. Admit it to yourself: you're just a cheap crook, like all the people you've been chasing around from day one.* As LP padlocked his bike to a pole outside the gift store, the devil on one shoulder and the angel on the other just kept talking into his ears. He wished they would get lost and take the money with them.

As he entered the store, LP was surprised by the large amount of merchandise in the sizable place. They had tons of items, large and small things you wouldn't find anywhere else. It looked like just the place some people would head for if they had ten dollars or less burning a hole in their pocket.

It was early in the day, and he didn't see another customer in the store. Sitting near the entrance behind the cash register was a pleasant-looking lady who was probably about the same age as Mr. Richards. She was most likely his wife.

She welcomed him saying, "If I can help you find anything, please ask. That is what I'm here for."

LP thanked her and mentioned he was just killing a little time and hoped she wouldn't mind if he just shopped around a bit. There was everything you could think of on the many shelves. They were primarily imports and low-cost items. LP noted that there was a stairway to the second floor at the rear of the store. That would lead to the area where Richards kept his secrets.

LP wanted to hear a bit of conversation from the owner, so he asked her if she had any large knitting bags. He said his mother had been after him to find her a nice big one.

The graceful lady said, "Yes, we have a big selection of bags near the rear of the store. Let me help you find what you're looking for. I'm sure we can find something she will enjoy."

There he viewed a variety of what he was looking for. Included in the selection were several large, colorful bags that looked exactly like the one Margareta had lugged around on her arm. This must have been where Margareta had found her bargain. The price was right, and LP decided to make the big purchase. Mom would love it, or LP could use it for a little stunt he wanted to try on Mr. Richards.

Before he left the store, LP talked briefly, and he could see the woman probably wasn't capable of being any kind of a criminal. He doubted she could commit any crime worse than jaywalking. It would be a stretch to include her in her husband's criminal life. Yes, he must have been a one-man show from start to finish.

LP had seen enough and headed back home with his ugly new bag. He planned to put it to work later. He was developing a master plan for Mr. Richards, the murderer.

LP returned his trusty old bike to the storage locker, and while he was there, he decided to rummage through some of his boxes of music to find a few CDs to have on hand. He wanted a little variety and some of his rare pets. In his travels he could listen to a little good music on his car radio or his portable CD player.

He had tons of the known, famous bands like Tommy Dorsey, Kenton, Basie, Woody Herman, Ellington, Glen Miller, and the like, but you heard them on the radio all the time. LP wanted to pick some good stuff, the rare—his pets. His tastes were out in left field somewhere. He couldn't explain his taste in music, but he had noticed that others often held their noses when exposed to his favorite ditties. He guessed that all people couldn't be on his planet. LP liked great musicians and unusual arrangements based on jazz or swing. Stuff disappeared when the Beetles came on the scene—lots of saxophones, good piano, and the thirteen-piece orchestra, all perfectly blended in a good arrangement.

He began to dig and pulled out a Nelson Riddle album called *Joy of Life*. It was happy music. Next he found a Floyd Cramer album for simple songs and a great piano style. He selected a Richard Claydeman solo piano CD entitled *The Carpenters*. He loved the Carpenters. Thomas Taltert's *Louisiana Suite* had to be included. *One Stormy Night* by the Mystic Moods was a definite winner. He had to have a Dodo Marmaroso bop piece. You almost had to take one of his just on his name. He was a master in jazz piano. Linda Ronstadt teamed up with Nelson Riddle on a three-disk CD entitled *Round Midnight* and hit a super-home run. Boyd Raeburn's 1945 band teamed up with Dizzy Gillespie on a tune called "Night in Tunisia" for the wildest of the wild. He made Stan Kenton sound tame. His record was entitled *March of the Boyds*. Another band similar to Kenton and Raeburn was Earle Spenser, who recorded about two albums before he disappeared. His music was extremely interesting, and it was a favorite of LP's. As a final item, LP had to include Peter Breiner, a European pianist and arranger. He had a symphonic pop orchestra, and on one of his LPs, he recorded a song entitled "Batman" and another entitled "Ja Da." The album title was *You Got a Friend*. Those old treasures just can't be topped. He gathered up his treasures and headed for home. He had about one week left to clean up his job, and tomorrow would be the beginning of a most interesting week.

CHAPTER 18

As LP walked through the back door at the probation office on Monday, he saw Shirley walking down the hall toward him. His first thought was that he believed she was right-handed, so if she tried to slap his face, it would be with her right hand. *Prepare to duck.*

This wasn't the case. Shirley said, "Hi, LP. I hope you enjoyed yourself as much as the rest of us did. I know I had fun."

LP smiled and answered, "I haven't had that much fun in a long time. I can take as much of that as you can dish out. But I know I owe you an apology for what I did. As I said before, the devil made me do it. Can we blame him?"

"Oh, forget that. Let's blame it on the booze."

"Okay," said LP, "let's blame it on the bossa nova then."

"Everyone enjoyed themselves. And you know what? Marjorie says she is in love with you and wants to marry you or at least have a date."

LP chuckled and said, "Come on, tell her to sober up and pick somebody her own age. Tell her to get back to her old boyfriend and fast."

"She will be heartbroken, LP, when I tell her. She was beginning to make big plans for you."

LP shook his head and said, "No. That's not in my plans. Anyway, this old bull has his eye on a little heifer out in another pasture."

"I see. And who might that be?"

LP paused briefly and looked to his left and to his right and back straight at Shirley, and with a silly grin on his face, he answered, "Don't you know?"

Shirley remained silent for a moment, and just as LP had done, she looked to her left and then to her right and back at LP, and as she pushed him lightly with both hands to his chest, she said, "Oh, LP Cinch, you dog."

LP could think of nothing to say except "Woof, woof."

Both laughed at their little exchange.

Then Shirley said, "Listen to me, Mr. Cinch. Let's get serious. We are planning another party for next Friday night, and you have to come or it will be a flop. I'll water the booze to keep the party from getting out of hand like the other night."

"Sounds good to me, and if I come, I'll promise to behave myself, or maybe you prefer that I don't behave. I might even drop a bottle or two in the punch when nobody is looking." LP added, "It would be nice if you could get a few more bodies to show up. Spread the wealth or something like that. More people, more clowns. Let somebody else take the stage besides me."

Shirley said, "More people, more fun? Not necessarily. I was thinking fewer people would make it better. Fewer is better sometimes, don't you think?"

LP replied, "Oh." Then suddenly the suggestion seeped into his vacant brain, and he added a drawn-out, "Ohhhh. I think I see what you mean—I hope. You know what? You can mark me down as definitely being there early Friday evening. And if you don't mind, I'll bring along a couple of my favorite CDs. They may tickle your fancy a bit."

LP went on, "I don't think I've ever told anyone this, but I've had a longtime secret ambition, and I'm fearful it may never come to pass. I'm down to my last few days here."

"What's the big ambition? I hesitate to ask."

"I've always wanted to kiss a probation officer, but I could never find a suitable subject. What do you think? None of these guys in here appeal to me in the slightest. And time is running out for me, so I'll just have to press on and keep my fingers crossed."

Shirley shook her head and replied, "Don't let your dream die, sonny boy. Rome wasn't built in a day." They both parted with smiles on their faces.

LP thought to himself, *Maybe my big plan to leave town in a big hurry isn't such a good idea after all. When things are going good, you don't want to fumble the ball. Go on the attack.* Step one was to remember to get to a store and buy a decent swimsuit, and then he could figure out the next move.

As soon as LP got settled at his desk, Jack Bothwell stuck his head around the corner and said, "Hey, Cinch, can you spare a minute in my office?"

LP couldn't think of anything he might've fouled up on lately, but you never know. He complied and sat down in front of the boss's desk.

Jack said, "Your replacement can't be in today. He has another training day, I would guess. However, he will be in tomorrow. How is he doing? I've had little time to sit down with him with you running him all around in the field. You've been keeping busy."

"Boss, you've got a good one. He will do very well, and the fact that he was chasing juveniles all around in the hall will help him out with that bunch he has in his caseload. He has a good attitude, and he really wants to be here. I've given him a written list of the thirty or so commandments on surviving. Mainly I told him a few basic things—like if you don't know what to do or are in doubt, then talk to your supervisor and listen to him. I told him he's not a social worker. He works for the court. Verify everything. Probationers lie. Cover your ass and your boss's ass at all times. Work hardest early in the month. Time is precious, and you won't have to worry about your monthly statistical reports later. And things like that.

"I find it very amusing to watch some of the POs around here every month. The first couple weeks of each month, you can see them sitting around the office, doing nothing but drinking coffee or whatever, but later in the month, they are frantically racing here and there, trying to see the people they should've chased down much earlier. It's the same every month. I guess there are no two people with the same priorities. I could never figure that out. My motto has been 'Do it now, not later. Nobody is going to do it for you.'"

Jack said, "It sounds like you are getting Lamond off on good footing. I can only hope he will be as good a worker as you have been. Now, before Wednesday, what I need from you is your badge. Nobody gets to keep their badge when they leave, and don't tell me you lost yours. All you guys want to hang on to those badges for life. They may give you yours on a plaque. They do that sometimes."

LP said, "I'll turn the thing in today. I never use it."

"I'll repeat," said Jack, "I hate to see you leave, but you know what you're doing. You can come here anytime you feel the urge or get lonesome for us. The back door is always unlocked. Just walk in. You said you didn't want a farewell dinner or any of that, but I think someone is cooking up a short get-together for Friday morning in the typing room. It will likely be cupcakes and soda. The director will probably make a rare appearance to give you a friendly pat on the back, a kick in the pants, and a final shove out the door. You might compose a speech, if you wish. Okay?"

LP got his badge out of his desk drawer, placed it on Jack's desk, and took a quote out of the movie *The Treasure of the Sierra Madre*, saying, "Today I got to show you my stinking badges."

The new PO wasn't going to be around, and that was just what the doctor ordered for LP. He had to conduct a little but very important rehearsal in the new PO's absence. Don Lamond would be present for act two. Tomorrow he had to be present for the plan to work.

LP wanted to get out in the field early and see as many faces as possible. His first stop would be the most important, though. He wanted to see Earle and his famous dog, Biff, along with his two other silent partners, Barbara and Phil.

It was still early, and they were home and as hospitable, as always. LP had decided earlier to break one of his strict rules: bribery. Earlier he had stopped at a local McDonald's and picked up a dozen and a half of their cheapest hamburgers.

LP said, "I brought all of you and Biff a little something for breakfast. I hope you like McDonald's." The smell filled the tiny residence. LP thought he could see every mouth, including Biff's, beginning to drool. Immediately everyone was chomping away on the feast.

"Don't forget to save a couple of those for Biff," LP suggested. Biff agreed. No question about it—these folks and dog approved of McDonald's.

After a couple of bites, Earle confirmed that nothing had changed since LP's earlier visit. He did report that they had gotten two letters from Al Capone Jr. so far.

"That's two hundred dollars," said Earle, "and like you told us, we didn't spend much of it. We just take a little when we really need it."

Soon the smelly bag and sandwich wrappers covered the floor. Biff was sniffing around, making sure nothing eatable was missed. LP assumed rightly that his treat was okay.

After loosening everybody up, LP wanted to get down to the important stuff. He told the gathering that he desperately needed their help. They could be of great service to law and order.

They all focused on LP as he said, "I think I know who killed Margareta. Richards did it. And if we don't do something, he is going to get away with it. We don't want that to happen, do we? Of course not. You told me that you think Richards was selling drugs in the neighborhood. For some reason, he killed Margareta over that.

"Tomorrow I plan to bring your new probation officer out here to see you. That way you can get along with him real good after I'm gone. The thing is, he doesn't know anything about any of this. Don't say a word about any money or seeing Margareta putting money where you found it. If he finds out about that, you guys are sunk. The cops will be all over you and probably Al Capone Jr. too. You won't have a prayer of keeping out of jail for some part of what went on. You'll be dead meat. As long as nobody hears anything about that stuff, you are in the clear, and you won't be accused of killing Margareta. Shut up and the mob will be happy. On top of that, the money will keep rolling in.

"Okay. Let's review. Tomorrow I come back. Act like you haven't seen me for quite a while. We talk a while, and then I ask Earle a question. I say, 'Earle, didn't you tell me that there must be some drug traffic going on at the souvenir store?' And then you say yes, and you might add that a lot of strange people are hanging around there lately. Barbara, you and Phil don't say a word; just listen.

"Earle, when you say yes to what I ask, then I will have about four people who say drugs are being pushed out of that store. I can then call the police and tell them what the new probation officer and I heard from a lot of other people. Hopefully the cops will raid that store and catch Richards with some of that stuff in the store. They also might be able to figure out who killed Margareta if they find the right gun in the store.

"And don't worry; the new probation officer and I will tell the cops we can't give them your names because you are our secret sources. Nobody will ask you anything because we won't give them your names. They will just have to accept the information from me and the new guy and go from there. Can you remember all of that?"

Earle nodded his head and said, "Sure, Mr. Cinch, don't worry. I won't mess it up."

"Good. We'll be out here early tomorrow, and you just answer the questions I ask." Before leaving, LP added, "Don't say anything about any McDonald's hamburgers either. I'm not supposed to be a good guy. I don't want that information to get around."

As LP drove off, he felt confident the little plan would succeed. Now he was going to break one of his golden rules. He was going to buy a swimsuit on company time. He was near a KMart and decided he would go for nothing but the best. If he drove halfway across town to the Macy's in the mall, he would have to pick only from the latest styles. But he didn't want to buy anything that looked like biblical David's pebble sling. He wanted something a little more old fashioned and with a lot more coverage. He made a quick shot into the store and was out and gone in minutes. He had found just what he was looking for. *Friday night, here I come!*

CHAPTER 19

Early on Tuesday morning, LP and Don Lamond hit the bricks in search of adventure. LP had a hunch he was in for a full day of answers to the big puzzle. LP would be working more than eight hours today, and he wanted to see Richards later in the day after Lamond had gone home.

The first stop of the day would be to the shanty of Earle Swope and his roommates, as LP had planned yesterday. He knew the three would be expecting him. On the way, LP gave Don a rundown on Earle and his lifestyle. Don would be seeing something a little north of normal. He explained to Don that he wanted to show him how to find Earle's house because he might have a hard time finding the place otherwise.

LP and Don were in luck. All three and dog were awake and dressed when they went through the gate to the cabin. "This is the place," said LP. They all gathered on the tiny porch.

LP explained to Don, "Earle is the unofficial mayor of the boulevard, and his friends here, Barbara and Phil, are his assistants. Biff is their bodyguard."

As coached, the three offered no conversation but grinned at LP's description of their honorary position. Biff didn't get it and ignored the humor. LP explained that Don would be coming by just as he had been doing in the past.

LP commented to Don, "If you want to find out what's going on out at the boulevard, just ask Earle and his pals."

LP looked back at Earle and asked, "Earle, how is the aluminum can business doing lately?"

Earle responded, "It's good when it's hot out like it has been lately, but you have to get out early and you have to know where to look."

Don asked, "What are you getting for cans nowadays, Earle?"

"A couple places are paying about sixty cents a pound."

LP calculated for a minute and said, "Let's see, twenty four cans to the pound, so you get about two and a half cents a can. Not bad. I better start picking them up when I see any laying around. But don't worry; I won't raid any of your area right here on the Boulevard."

LP changed the subject and said, "I was explaining to Don that I had heard from people around here that there seemed to be a lot of drug activity down the street around the souvenir store. As a matter of fact, I think you guys told me that you saw some of that going on down there. Wasn't that you?"

Earle took the opening. "Yes, we all noticed a few of those types going in and out of the store lately. They didn't look like regular shoppers from around here."

LP responded, "I feel like telling the sheriff's department that they ought to keep an eye out for that kind of stuff. We don't want the boulevard to go to the dogs with that. There are a lot of kids living around here."

LP had the information now officially and wanted to get going to the next place on his list. He said, "We have a lot of work to do today. Don has the same phone number as mine in case you want to report anything."

Don said, "Here, Earle, I'll give you my card with my phone number on it."

As LP followed Don through the gate, he looked back at Earle and gave him a big okay, holding his arm up and making a circle with his thumb and forefinger making a big circle. Earle nodded and smiled.

When they got into the car, LP said, "Regarding Earle, when you see his lifestyle, it's easy to look down on him, one way or another. You know what, though, I doubt if he looks down on anybody or himself. He doesn't have to. I never heard him gripe about anything because he is too busy living the life he has chosen, and he is happy with it. Did you notice that Biff didn't look neglected or hungry? Earle depends on no one, and he is guiding along a couple of other people who seem to need a little guidance. He has nothing to be ashamed of, and we all should probably turn our judgments on ourselves now and then.

"You heard what Earle said. There's dope flying around these here parts, and it's time to call in the law. I think I'm going to slip a deputy I know a message that everybody out here knows that something is going on. If the cops ask who said that, I'm going to tell them I'm not a squealer. They can take it or they can ignore it. It's up to them. But my hope is they don't ignore it."

Just before noon, after hitting a number of probationers, LP said he had gotten a phone call from a guy in the caseload with a change of address. He was moving out of his apartment and said he was planning to move in with his girlfriend.

"Let's go see him at the new address. He's on probation for child molesting. I hate all those people. These types you have to watch like a hawk. Most of them are really pretty slick and can't be trusted."

Mr. Herbert Thompson, the molester, was at the new address when they arrived. LP introduced the man to Don and explained that he would be taking over the man's supervision next week. Everyone walked into the living room area, where the man's girlfriend was sitting. In the corner of the room were two little girls seated at a small table having a tea party.

The lady commented, "These are my two daughters, Mary and Ruby."

Immediately it was evident that there was a huge problem that had to be resolved without any delay. LP said, "Ma'am, I understand that Mr. Thompson wants to move in with you, but if he does, he will be in violation of his probation. You know we are probation officers, and Mr. Thompson is on probation. Did he tell you why he is on probation?"

"Yes, he said he was on probation for getting too friendly with a couple of children, but he won't do it again."

"Ma'am, you're right. He is a convicted child molester. He molests little boys and girls. And you have your two daughters living here with you. Probation says no way to that. We don't care what he says. The court says he can't be in contact with children of any age. I have to check the court order at our office, but I am certain it says he is not allowed to be in contact with any minors. His order may say he can only be around children when he is accompanied by a responsible adult. I realize you may be a responsible adult, but you can't be with your daughters every day, twenty-four hours a day. It's impossible. Every night you have to sleep. You may have to go out into your backyard to hang clothes on the clothesline, you may run over to see the neighbor for a minute or cook dinner. There will be many, many times when you are not face-to-face with your children. And where will Mr. Thompson be when that happens? Will he behave when you aren't around? You won't know. You have to realize that. He may tell you he won't do anything like he has done in the past, but you've got to understand that he is a molester and he can't help himself. The court knows that, and they are not going to budge on what they ordered."

In a pleading voice, the lady responded, "But we love each other, and I want him here. He's promised he won't get into trouble again. I need his help here."

"Ma'am, why do guys like this always seek out gullible ladies and pull this business? Your children are at stake here. Give that a serious thought. Are you willing to risk their safety just because he says he will be good? I bet you a dollar to a doughnut that if you don't let him move in, he will disappear very quickly. He'll look for greener pastures."

LP turned his attention to Mr. Thompson. "Sir, I don't know how you assess your problem with children, but the court has it figured out. You are putting yourself in a very vulnerable position. Can you trust yourself? You pull your little stunt one more time, and I can assure you that you will be living a long time behind bars. Molesters aren't very popular with hardened criminals doing time in prison. They're known to hand out a lot of special punishment for molesters. They don't like them because many of them were molested when they were children."

LP could see these two people were not budging on the moving-in plan. The woman continued to use the approach that they could work out a sensible plan.

She said, "I never let them out of my sight."

LP countered, "That's impossible. Dream on."

He continued, "Sir, don't move in here. I am going to check that probation order again, and I am going to discuss this with my supervisor. Ma'am, if he is here after today, you better have your eyes on him all of the time. You know you've been warned, and if we find any evidence that anything is happening that shouldn't be going on, even though you have committed no crime yet, you could be charged with child neglect and other crimes if anything—anything at all—happens to the girls. I will be coming back here as soon as I have talked to my boss. We will see you in a day or two. Hopefully by then you will both have come to your senses. As of now, Thompson, you are just a visitor, and your girlfriend has her eyeballs on you every second you're here."

LP and Don got up and left. LP explained, "I want to go back to the office right away. You can't pussyfoot around with people like that. You have to draw a very clear picture; otherwise you might end up with egg on your face. And if you give them an inch, they will take a mile."

On their way back to the office, LP gave Don a rundown on several molesters he had supervised.

"They live in another world. Many are almost like sociopaths. I've had a few of those too. They will drive you crazy until you figure out where they are coming from. With sociopaths, their behavior is antisocial, and they lack a sense of moral responsibility or social conscience. At least that's what the dictionary says. They lie to you, and they will jive you around until you figure out who you are dealing with. Many of the molesters are the same way, and they live in their dream world. Most have no guilt for their actions.

"I had a child molester assigned to me who could be noted for what you might expect from that type. After this guy was assigned to me, in less than one month he called me on the phone to ask if he could take two of his nephews camping with him for a weekend. He explained that there would just be him and the two boys. They would be up in the tree country and would be camping out in a tent. As calmly as I could contain myself, I asked for the names of the boys. After he gave the names and their ages, which were in grade school, I tried to calm myself down a bit so I could explain the facts of life to the man. I told him, 'My friend, you are a molester. You are a convicted molester, you molest little boys, and the court forbids you from any such contact with juveniles. An exception might be if another adult who is aware of your conviction is present at all times and is completely aware that you molest little boys. Then it might be a possibility. In this case, however, I'm telling you that you better not go anywhere with those boys. This camping trip is cancelled. I assume that the parents of these children are aware of your court status. I plan to call them and draw a graphic picture of your dopey plan. Have you got it?'

"He agreed to cancel the camping trip, and I told him, 'Very good, because I am following up on this.' This probationer seemed not to realize where he was landing himself and the children because of his denial of the truth."

LP continued, "I had a guy who was convicted of molesting, and I was assigned to prepare the pre-sentence report for the court. The man was in the county jail when I got information from him. He was a little, harmless-looking man and wasn't constrained about expressing his feelings. He knew he was a molester and was trying to justify his acts. He said he liked to play spin the bottle with little girls he knew. A harmless game. He said his behavior wasn't any different than that of the rulers in ancient Rome and other important people of the past. They molested children, and the society apparently tolerated it. He felt that this gave him a license to do as they had. It made me think his twisted logic could be compared to John Dillinger. He robbed banks. He was famous. Then why isn't robbing banks acceptable conduct? I imagine that today my little, harmless-looking man is happily sitting somewhere in his prison cell playing spin the bottle with his cell mate."

When Don and LP got back to the office, they sat down in Jack Bothwell's office and explained that they had just left a probationer on probation for molesting. LP explained, "We have a big problem on the horizon. The man wants to move in with a new girlfriend who just happens to have two preschool-aged daughters. Does that sound familiar? True love. He probably introduced himself to her in the last week or so in a grocery store when he spotted her with the girls. Or maybe in the park where the mother took the girls to play. You know the old story.

"And as usual, when I explained the man's status to the woman, she swept all that aside. She found a new boyfriend and to heck with the facts. She said he told her he was on probation, but she apparently believed his lies. She said she knew he wouldn't be harmful to the girls because he loved her and the girls. We told Mr. Molester that what he told her was a crock and he can't move in and to dump that plan completely. I don't think they are going to cooperate at all. I told them I was going to report all of this to you for total clarity on this nutty arrangement. We explained to Mr. Molester that at this point he better not move in and Mrs. Gullible had better not leave those girls out of her sight for a minute. I told them that we would be back out there after we talked to you."

Jack looked up at the ceiling for a moment—maybe he was searching for divine help—and then said, "We need to arrange for both parties, and the little girls, if necessary, to come into the office, and we will all sit down and review the matter."

"Fine with me," said LP. "Don got here just in time for the fireworks. I'll call them now and will tell them to get in here Friday morning, and we will be waiting."

By the time LP and Don left Jack's office, it was nearing lunchtime. LP had to do something important on his lunch hour and told Don he would be back in the office in an hour. It was time to get organized on a plan to solve this murder business. A little trap had to be set for Mr. Richards.

LP drove to Red's place on the boulevard, a perfect place to set the trap. Red had an ancient feed store where you could get chicken feed and seeds. He also sold fish bait and fishing tackle. There were always a few people in the store talking about fishing and things in general.

As far as LP was concerned, it was one of his favorite places to get a good, cold bottle of soda on a hot day. In the store was an old-fashioned ice chest filled with all flavors of soda. On the side of the chest was a bottle cap remover for immediate drinkers. One of LP's favorites was cream soda, but there were many choices. In front of the store was a long wooden bench that was usually occupied by customers smoking or having a soda and talking over world affairs.

LP walked in and dug out a cream soda. As he paid for the drink, he asked Red how late the store stayed open.

"We close at six o'clock p.m. every day, and we're closed on Sundays," answered Red.

As he sipped his drink, LP walked outside and strolled to the driveway at the side of the building. He casually looked beyond the open gate to check the big lot behind the building. He could see a lot of empty parking spaces as well as several stacks of pallets along the back fence. Close to the gate was a Dumpster close to a side fence. A few cardboard boxes were stacked near and on top of the Dumpster. *This will be perfect*, thought LP.

This is where he hoped to spring his trap. He would send Mr. Richards a little invitation.

LP turned in his empty soda bottle and headed back to work. He would be back at Red's after dark.

CHAPTER 20

Through all of LP's serious thoughts, he knew there was no question of who killed Margareta. It had to have been Richards, but LP wanted to try something that would establish that without any doubt. At the same time, LP didn't want to get himself directly or indirectly involved in Richards' arrest. He wanted to just be an unknown spectator.

LP decided to make his home contact with Richards at about six in the evening, shortly before dark. Richards was usually home at that time after his workday at the air force base. LP's plan was to plant some seeds in Richards' mind that would lead to a pretty good case of self-incrimination. If the plan worked, it would be like a large, evil bug getting stuck in a huge sheet of fly paper. No escape.

LP knew Richards would give anything to get his money or drugs back. The thing was that Richards didn't know for certain if Margareta had completed the sale as directed. After Margareta got caught by her boss with no money or drugs, Richards had been mightily upset. He wanted one or the other. Margareta might have said she'd received the money but it got lost when she hid it. But Richards really didn't know what went on that evening. Margareta might have lied to him just to throw him off and then keep the dough for herself. Actually, Richards could have figured out that Margareta actually did get the money; otherwise Richards' partner in crime, Ray Linn, would have gotten back to him to find out why Margareta didn't show up with the drugs. Linn got his drugs and hit the road.

LP's plan would get Richards' blood flowing pretty well, he hoped. And if Richards did get sucked into LP's plan, it would prove Richards was the head man and the one who would be the big loser without that payoff. He would be the only one who had a reason for killing Margareta, the double crosser in his mind.

LP would have to do a little fibbing again—no serious lies but far enough from the truth to get this plan rolling. He knew Margareta had been picked up that night after the exchange. LP was going to tell Richards that while Margareta was briefly in custody, she made a telephone call to her downtown roommate, Don Darcy, with an interesting but confusing message with some instructions the roommate and LP couldn't figure out. This would get the ball rolling. Actually, the roommate got no message from Margareta, and LP didn't get any information whatsoever from the roommate. It would all be fiction, but Richards wouldn't know the difference.

Shortly after six p.m., LP parked in front of Richards' residence. He was in luck. Richards was sitting out on the front porch having a cool one. As usual, he looked sober and congenial. He had the appearance of a hardworking family man.

LP wanted to disarm Richards a little before he got to his plan. He'd try to get Richards to believe LP might be somewhat of an ally or friend. After a short discussion of the weather, LP asked, "You haven't been pawning anything since you got on probation, have you? There's no law against that, but I was just curious."

"No, I certainly haven't. I learned my lesson, and that won't happen again."

LP continued, "There's nothing wrong with pawning something, but always make certain you aren't dumping anything that's stolen, especially if the victim can identify the thing later. I guess you know now that the pawn shops have to detail everything pawned and give the list to the cops monthly. And the cops can match a lot of things that are stolen."

"I guess when you buy something like that, you better not pawn it or even get rid of it."

"Oh, you can get rid of it, but avoid the pawn shops."

"How then?" asked Richards.

"If you buy something you are not sure of, sell it to the type of person you bought it from. Like another crook. You won't get top price, but you probably can still make a profit. Or try a fence."

Richards looked somewhat interested now. LP continued, "If the cops run the item down and it is connected with a crime, the man who buys it from you will have to take the fall. The cops will check his record and decide he is just another burglar. They will charge him with that. If he says he bought it from somebody else, he can't win because they can still get him for receiving stolen property. He's guilty either way. And one thing about criminals—they hate squealers. It wouldn't be profitable for the guy to expose you. He is still going to jail for receiving. Why take on an added tag as a squealer?

"If you're going to sell something, make sure the people you buy it from have nothing to hide—hopefully people you know."

Richards acted as if he was in agreement with LP's pearls of wisdom. How could he disagree? LP didn't want to give Richards a class on how to be a better criminal because he wouldn't be. If things went as planned, Richards wouldn't be available for anything for a long time.

After his extended lecture on fencing stolen goods, LP wanted to get the conversation turned to the subject of Margareta. It was time to get back to brass tacks.

He began his move. "It's a small world. I didn't realize it at first, but one of your wife's employees was on my caseload a while back."

Richards nodded and replied, "Oh, I bet you mean Margareta Gonzales. She told my wife when she started working for us that she was on probation for taking somebody's money from their wallet. She said it was a very small amount of money, so we gave her a chance. My wife is so kindhearted that she can't say no to anyone. When she asked for the job, my wife said we could use some part-time help stacking shelves and moving crates around in the back room. We couldn't let her work up in front waiting on customers with her walking around in dresses.

"She just got in a few hours a week. She was a good worker, and I think she liked her job. Margareta seemed very secure in his belief that he wasn't a man. And you had to respect his beliefs. I would think he had a very difficult time with his situation. He told us he had a plan to have an operation someday. Perhaps if he had dressed a lot less noticeably than he did, he might have been able to fit into society a lot better. But he made his choice, and we tried to let him be the way he felt most comfortable. We didn't see anything about a funeral in the newspaper. Have you seen anything about that?"

"I understand the family had no money at all for a funeral, but some church group heard about the financial problem and aided them with the total cost of the services. I think she was buried at a small cemetery somewhere down the river a ways. So, did you know that she got bumped off?"

"Yes. When she didn't show up for a couple days, we called her mother, who told us that she had gotten killed. We were shocked."

"Yes," said LP, "it's hard to figure out why it ended up that way. Margareta seemed so harmless and friendly with everyone."

"That's the way she was at work too," said Richards. "Did the police ever find out who did it?"

"No. Not a word. Not a clue. Did the police come out and talk to you or your wife?"

"No, I don't think they knew she worked here part-time, and by the time we heard about it, four or five days had gone by. We decided her working here didn't have anything to do with a murder, so we never called them."

"I don't think the police are wasting a lot of time solving her death. I had only been his PO for a very short time before he moved downtown. He was on probation for ripping off drunks in his spare time and probably picked the wrong mark to get some money, and that ended Margareta. She hung around in a very rough part of town, and things like that happen every so often. The killer could be one of many people and likely someone Margareta didn't even know—someone who didn't like a man in woman's clothes."

Richards agreed. "You're like me. You call Margareta her and then him. It's totally confusing. A man with a woman's name."

"Yes indeed," said LP, "and he was difficult to supervise because he kept running back and forth from his mother's house to his roommate's place downtown. He was downtown mostly, so we transferred her to another officer. After the murder, out of curiosity, I called his roommate downtown to see if he had any idea why Margareta got shot. The roommate said he had no idea why it happened. He said the last time he had heard from Margareta was a couple days before the killing. It was a confusing phone call from Margareta asking for help.

"The roommate told me that Margareta called him from the sheriff's office downtown and said she got picked up for some reason. She didn't know when they were going to let her go. She didn't do anything to get picked up, but the main reason she said she called was to ask a favor. She said, 'If they don't release me by morning, please go over behind Red's place on the boulevard and look in the back parking lot behind some stacked-up pallets next to the fence and get my bag that I hid there. You know what it looks like. It's full of some stuff I'll explain later. Hang on to it, and don't tell anybody about it. What's in it isn't mine. I'll explain about it when I get out.'"

Now LP wanted to bait the hook. He could see Richards was absorbing and analyzing every word of the fairy tale. He said, "The roommate told me he went over to the jail the next morning and they told him Margareta wasn't in jail. Margareta had been released at six o'clock that morning. They just wanted to question him on something. But the roommate said Margareta didn't come by or call, so he decided he better go look for the bag as Margareta had requested. He drove up and down the boulevard looking for Red's place but couldn't find it anywhere on the boulevard, so he went back home empty-handed."

LP held his breath and hoped Richards was putting two and two together. He hoped Richards made the connection the roommate didn't make. Since the roommate didn't live in that part of town, he didn't know there was no Red's place. However, there was a store on the boulevard with the name of Southtown Feed and Grain that is owned by Red Wilson. Everybody living in the area called it Red's, which was a no-brainer. Red's was the place you headed for on any hot afternoon if you wanted the best bottle of ice-cold soda in town and a place to share it with friends. It was certain in LP's mind that Richards had made the connection. He had grown up in this part of town, and additionally, when LP mentioned the back lot of Red's, Richards appeared to want to say something but at the last instant held his tongue. He didn't want to let the cat out of the bag. He knew where his bag of money was. LP could see that the fish had bought the whole goofy story.

LP wanted to get out of there. He acted like he hadn't figured out Margareta's riddle. He had mentioned that he didn't know the boulevard like a lot of the old-timers. He said he was getting hungry and was going to call it a day.

It was getting dark, and LP had to make some fast moves. He had his eight hours in on the job, so now he was officially on his own time. He wanted this little adventure to work out.

He headed back to Red's place and parked his car around the corner, where it would be out of sight. Red's was already closed for the day, and the side gate was wide open, as always.

He knew the layout of the backyard pretty well, having glanced at it earlier. At the far rear of the lot was a big stack of pallets against the back fence. He would hide the purse behind that stack but close enough to be reached by hand. LP didn't want Richards to strain himself when he grabbed his prize.

Near the entrance, just past the gate was a rusty, battered Dumpster resting close to the side fence. There were a few empty cardboard boxes lying on top of the thing and a few more on the ground close by. The Dumpster was about three feet from the fence. That was perfect. He had just enough space to be able to get behind the Dumpster and still view everything in the lot. He found a small wooden box in the pile of trash that made a perfect chair. LP figured it might be a long night if Richards didn't come running to get his lost money.

Before LP took his post, he arranged several of the nearby boxes on top of the Dumpster so he could look around when standing and would not be seen by the visitor. It was now getting dark enough that nobody would notice anything fishy going on in the yard.

LP relaxed in his hiding place. It was just him and that big, ugly purse he had bought a week earlier at Richards' store. He didn't even have to dig up Margareta's original purse. In the new bag were a local phone book and several magazines for good measure. It was just about the right weight to make it look like the real McCoy. He had one little item in his pocket he planned to use if all went well: his camera. He pulled it out and got it ready. It was a cheap thirty-five-mm flash camera, and it never failed. He hoped to get the sucker's picture holding that worthless bag of paper. He had no idea what the point of the photo was, but who knows? A picture is worth a thousand words. It would come in handy if he ever wanted to write a book about this phase of his life. One thousand words must be five or six pages, at least. That could come in quite handy if he was at a loss for words.

The wait gave LP time to think of the big change coming up in his life. He didn't know what he was going to do. He had joked about all the dopey jobs he could get, but he knew he had to get serious about something worth doing. One thing he wanted to pursue was a job where he could be his own boss. No more orders from headquarters. That was the problem was with things these days—headquarters. People couldn't get a chance to think for themselves.

Suddenly he heard someone coming his way. He was surprised. He had only been sitting there for less than an hour and a half, and here came his first customer. LP hoped Richards hadn't sent a flunky to get the purse. He could hear the crunching on the gravel, closer and closer. A flashlight swept the yard and then focused on the stack of pallets at the back of the yard. LP peeked around several of the boxes in front of him. His eyes were accustomed to the dark. He watched the flashlight beam move to the back of the yard. Whoever it was knew exactly where to go. LP knew he had his man. It was Richards. Old dopey had swallowed the bait, hook, line, and sinker.

Richards searched around briefly, bent down, and pulled the bag out. He set the bag down on the concrete and started digging around in it. At the same time, LP stepped out from behind the Dumpster, camera in hand, and fired off a quick shot. The flash probably blinded Richards for a split second, but by that time, LP was halfway out of the lot and gaining altitude. A split second later, LP heard a gunshot go off, and the round slammed into the side of the building just a couple of feet from his head. By now LP was breaking the world record for the hundred-yard dash. He rounded the corner and was still picking up speed as he got to his car. He never looked back—not once. And he almost burned rubber as he sped away.

The plan worked. Richards was plenty mad now after looking at that worthless phonebook. Richards would fully realize that he had been set up, and his involvement in all of this was now an open book. This exercise proved without a doubt that Richards was in the middle of it. It also verified something else: the man had a weapon and was willing and able to use it. He was probably holding the gun that had murdered Margareta when LP outran the shot.

LP had planned to call law enforcement in the morning at work, but he now realized Richards wasn't going to stand around and do nothing. If he had anything to hide, like drugs, guns, or anything dealing with the death of Margareta, he would be getting all of that as far away from his home and his place of business as fast as he could. As soon as LP got home tonight, he was going to call the sheriff's office and talk to or leave a message for Officer Hal Schaefer. Schaefer was the officer LP had talked to earlier when they wanted information on the residence of Ray Linn, who was now in the county jail awaiting his trial.

LP headed straight home and dug up the phone number. Schaefer wasn't available, but an officer who worked with him took LP's message. LP explained who he was and said he had provided Officer Schaefer earlier with information on a successful drug bust. LP didn't want to get into all of the details and said, "Hopefully, this information will get into the hands of Officer Schaefer as soon as possible. I've had four different probationers on my caseload who have given me some details of lots of drug sales occurring out of a store on the boulevard owned by John Richards. Hopefully Schaefer will wish to give this some priority because I also was alerted that Richards might have been tipped off from some other source that his dealings were going to be reported to authorities. Richards could be preparing for any investigation of his activities."

LP provided the officer with the address of the store and Richards' residence. He added that Richards' wife, who was the co-owner or sole owner of the store, didn't appear to be involved in the drug sales.

LP decided to give a few details for the officer to get the whole picture. "You know where there's smoke there is usually fire. Richards is on probation for receiving stolen property. Some doper probably exchanged stolen goods for drugs, and Richards tried to pawn the stuff. Now he is on probation. Richards has several avenues of getting drugs—good drugs. His store has to get most of their inventory shipped in from Asia. Possibly there's some smuggling there. Richards is some sort of civilian mechanic for the air force and gets sent out into the Pacific several times a year on temporary assignments. He travels on the military planes. I don't think they fool with customs. Do they? Anyway, he has lots of ways to bring in drugs."

But most importantly, LP wanted to include the important details regarding Margareta's murder in the message. "Of note," he said, "Margareta Fred Gonzales was murdered about a month ago in Two Rivers and was an employee at Richards' store. It is possible Gonzales was killed by Richards over some issue, probably drugs. Richards has been known to carry a handgun at times. If authorities recovered a bullet from the victim, Gonzales, it might match Richards' handgun or other guns he might own. Have Schaefer call me at probation if further details are needed. After this week, my caseload will be covered by Don Lamond at this same office. On Friday, I am retiring. I assume you record all phone calls, but if not, I will be around until Friday at five o'clock p.m. After that I'm gone. I'll be gone fishing. I don't know how hard it is to get a search warrant approved, but I believe it could be fruitful."

LP hoped that if and when Schaefer got back to probation about who the informants were that Lamond could avoid giving specific names. It wouldn't be the greatest sin that ever happened if he did spill the beans. LP had explained to Lamond that he wasn't going to stick his neck out and be a squealer. But if Lamond gave the names, that would be a good way to have all of the people he supervised clam up every time he came around. Then he would get nothing from them. There would be no more free tips for Lamond.

After LP finished the phone call, he began to feel pretty beat. He had run out of gas. It had been a pretty eventful evening—one that doesn't come along very often. He needed to get a good night's sleep, and then tomorrow he could grind to a stop. On Friday he would be able to pull the curtain on this business he'd been in for so long. He knew he needed to totally unwind and try to retrieve all of his marbles, if possible. Maybe they were gone forever. After a little rest, he could catch things as they came at him. No more than one thing at a time. Nevada would be first. He recalled the little plan he had made at Fred's place tonight. He'd probably dream about it all night long. He felt it was a worthy effort even though it was kind of a dopey, meaningless stunt—one that could even get you killed. Maybe Margareta Fred's murder might be avenged after all. And the photo he snapped—he'd just hang on to that. It might come in handy sometime down the road. Who knew?

CHAPTER 21

fter a good night's sleep, LP was ready for a day without fear or dread. At least that was what he hoped for. It was the day before retirement, and what could the world drop on him today? He didn't intend to make any more home contacts, and he would totally try to bluff the day away. Don wouldn't show up until after lunch, and LP could explain how to handle some of the mountains of paperwork in the afternoon. At this point, he began to empty his desk and tear down yellowing, outdated papers from the wall next to his desk. Without a doubt, these things no longer had any value, meaning, or relevance.

As the morning progressed, workers passed back and forth, and many had remarks about the retirement and said they would miss LP after he was gone. *Yeah,* LP said to himself, *by next Monday most will have forgotten my name.* But LP accepted their good wishes and knew he would never forget these folks and most of the unfortunate probationers they had all worked with. With the help of a lot of inspiration, he might even decide to write a book, poem, or something about these years in probation-ville. Not unless he was totally at a loss to do anything else, though.

LP decided that at lunchtime he wanted to satisfy his curiosity about something needed to be solved and then put in his past for good. He had a full hour to bring it to a conclusion instead of having any lunch.

At noon he cranked up the old car headed down the river road to Pearville. Fortunately, he was able to find the pastor of the church he had contacted a month earlier. He was the priest who had provided funeral services for Margareta.

The priest remembered LP and said, "Happy to see you, sir. You arranged the Fred Gonzales funeral. You made the family extremely happy, and the services were well attended. And two days ago the engraved monument was placed at the site. It is a very fitting marker."

LP said, "Well, I had very little to do with all of this and had nothing to do with the cost. They will be happy to hear of the favorable outcome. The reason I came by today was to find out where the cemetery is. Can you help me out on that?"

"I certainly can. I spend a lot of time there. The cemetery is less than a mile from here. You can't miss it. Go back toward Two Rivers and take a left turn, and then go less than a mile. The cemetery is on the left."

LP thanked the priest and followed instructions. As he drove into a small parking lot next to the road, he noted another car in the lot. Otherwise the area was completely devoid of humankind. There was total quiet except for the cackle of a pheasant in a field somewhere nearby. It was almost like paddling in the river; there was not a sound, not a soul, except maybe for the one in the graveyard.

As LP left his car, he saw several people in the small cemetery. He immediately recognized one of the people as Fred Gonzales' mother, Delores Gonzales, and a younger woman, possibly a daughter.

As he approached, he said to Mrs. Gonzales, "Hello, do you remember me?"

Delores responded, "I remember you, but I was told that if I was to see you again, I was to make like I don't know you. So no, I don't know you, Mr. Cinch."

LP laughed and said, "You did well, Mrs. Gonzales. Just keep it up."

The three were standing in front of the Gonzales area of the cemetery. Behind six small, granite gravestones, was a larger and more impressive one with the name Fred M. Gonzales carved on it. Besides the name, it had the dates of birth and death and the statement, "Rest in Peace." LP looked around the cemetery and noted that the new marker stood out and had a noble appearance. He looked at the two women and saw the happy smiles on their faces.

Mrs. Gonzales said, "Our prayers have been answered. Fred can truly, truly rest in peace now."

Mrs. Gonzales turned to the younger woman and said, "This is Maria, Fred's younger sister. She drove me here today to see the gravestone for the first time. She lives with me. We are so proud of her. She is so helpful. She has been an A student all through grade school and high school. This year she got all As at the junior college. And she works part-time too."

LP smiled and said, "All As all of the time—Maria, I am impressed. I don't think I ever got an A for anything all of the time I was in school. What are you trying to get in school? What is your interest?"

"I would like to teach, but it may take a long time. I am at the point where I should be taking upper-division classes. I need to get into Twin Rivers State College for those courses. I may have to skip school for a while and get a full-time job. The costs of school at State are much pricier."

"That would be bad news to interrupt your big hope. Keep that positive plan in mind. I finally got a degree after many interruptions, and a college degree is worth all the hard work along the way."

"Yes, I realize that," said Maria. "Right now my part-time job doesn't pay much, and most of what I make covers my car payment. It's the family transportation. Mom is so sweet to put up with me."

Mrs. Gonzales volunteered, "Maria is so much help for me. The family is going to help her get into State College somehow."

LP attempted to add some encouragement. "Well, if I come up with any ideas on better jobs or school grants or things of that nature, maybe I could call your mother and help you with school. If I could come up with some answers, Mrs. Gonzales, you could then officially make like you do know me. How does that sound?"

Mrs. Gonzales smiled and said, "Maria is a very determined young lady, and she has never given up on anything she set her goals to do. Our prayers will be answered."

LP looked at his watch and said, "I have to get back to work or I may get fired. Pray that I get back to work on time. It was great to see what those unknown people provided for Fred. I will tell them how happy all of you are with the results of the burial. I might do some additional begging while I have their ears. But I promise you nothing. In the meantime, keep making like you don't know me."

On his way back to work, LP was a bit fearful that his social worker spirit was trying to clutter up his mind again. He had to focus on reality and not jump into what was not his business. He was escaping from all that involvement with people, so he just had to cool it and let sleeping dogs lie.

When he got back to work, Don was sitting at his desk. LP said, "Well, after today that is going to be your headquarters. You can fill up the desk drawers. I cleaned out all my junk and all my secrets. You can officially fill the drawers with all of your valuables."

Later in the day, LP got an important telephone call. It was Mr. Molester, who was scheduled to come to the office the following week.

LP's favorite molester sounded a bit excited. That seemed a bit strange after the long-winded threats LP had thrown on him during the last home contact.

The caller said, "We're so happy. I think we solved the problem of my living with Hazel and the girls."

"Great," said LP. "It sounds like you got some new digs. I'm glad you came to your senses. That was the only answer to a big problem."

The man said, "No. We came up with a better solution. Yesterday morning we drove to Reno and got married. We just got back a couple of hours ago. We wanted you to be the first to know."

LP said, "You what? You got married? I can't believe I'm hearing this. If you had just moved out of there, we would have no problem. But now you two got married. I don't know how big of a problem it is, but I know I have never seen a bigger problem. When the judge hears this, it'll be like a volcano blowing its top. When my supervisor hears about it, it's going to be like two volcanoes going off at once. I have no idea how this is going to work out. I can't even guess. Now here is what I want you to do. I want you in here next week at the same time we arranged. Bring your bride and the children if you can't find a reliable babysitter. Bring with you any papers, wedding license, or evidence of this marriage that just happened in Nevada. The most important thing is for you to get in here as directed. I can't believe what you did has solved anything unless each of you elects to live in two different cities. That's something you might have considered."

After the call, LP thought of what he would have liked to have said to Mr. Boob. He would have liked to say to him, "I am certain you are going to enjoy your marriage even though you two will only be able to get together on visiting day at the prison. It's also very hard to kiss anyone through a glass window in the visitor's booth." But he didn't want to alarm the man unnecessarily before he came to the office.

Now LP would have to break the news to his boss, Jack Bothwell.

"Come on, Don," LP said as he clasped his palms together and looked aloft in a moment of silent prayer. "Let's go in and talk to the boss for a minute. This is one of those times when we go talk to the boss because we are stumped. Hang on to your hat. I don't know what is going to happen, but have you ever seen a volcano erupt?"

LP and Don walked in and sat down. Jack said, "Well, what's up? Have you changed your mind about retiring? I think they already bought the 7UP and cupcakes for tomorrow, so you can't back out of it now. Besides, I think Don is going to be an improvement around here."

"No, the retirement is still on, but boss, hold on to your chair. Our molester and his girlfriend just called. I told him to come in here on Monday, as we arranged, or we will go out there and drag him in here. He had a bit of news for us—his answer to the problem he is causing. He and his girlfriend got married yesterday in Reno. He figures that solves the little matter of his moving in with her and ending any threat to her little girls."

With a stunned looked on his face, Jack said, "They got married?"

LP replied, "That's exactly what I asked when he told me of this big, much-contemplated plan."

"They got married!" Jack repeated. "Where the hell do we go from here?"

With a crooked little smile on his face, LP answered, "It's wild, ain't it, boss? I could almost go back to my desk, get up on top of it, and dance an Irish gig for a half an hour or so. On Monday morning I will be long gone. Expect the unexpectable and the unbelievable. They come up with a new wrinkle every time. But this time I have outsmarted them. This time it's not my problem. On Monday morning I will be lying on a beach somewhere getting a tan. I am the happiest man in the world knowing I am getting out of this mad world for good. Nothing can top this."

Jack glumly responded, "But what about us?"

"You could join me on the beach. But seriously, one thing you could do is get rid of this case pronto. Transfer it to the intensive supervision unit. That's where it needs to be. The intensive case officers have about thirty cases to supervise while we have around one hundred and thirty cases most of the time. Intensive can go out there every day of the week if they want. Only it wouldn't resolve anything except your problem. Whoever ends up with this case should call Child Protection Services at the welfare department and get them involved. And I'd also call the county health nurses about it. Have them get in on the party too. I know you are way ahead of me on this, but it may end up back in court on some judge's desk. These molesters are the slipperiest bunch you can run in to. The little girls are not safe with that guy around. But, 'hallelujah, I'm a bum,' it's not my problem. I think the intensive caseload is the only way you and Don can live through this. Maybe if the guy doesn't show up on Monday, you could consider filing a violation of probation with the court, but that takes way too long. Somebody should be sitting on this guy's neck today, if not sooner."

After that meeting, LP just sat around the rest of the afternoon and chuckled now and then, thinking about Mr. Molester's greatest stunt ever. It was a real show stopper. And tomorrow wouldn't be just another day. It would be the final straw. It would be the day when they cut the shackles from LP. It would be a new day with new responsibilities and new opportunities. Who would be his new master? His hope would be that the new master's initials would be LP.

CHAPTER 22

t eight o'clock in the morning, LP was at his desk as usual, but this would be his final day. He decided he might have to go for a second cup of coffee because he was feeling a slight case of jitters coming on. He realized that if he was going to get his cupcake today and his pass to freedom, he would have to make some remarks at the festivities. Making speeches wasn't exactly his favorite pastime. As he analyzed himself, he believed he wasn't a talker and a teacher but more of a listener and a learner. When the boss asked him if he wanted a big farewell party with lunch at some local restaurant, LP had rejected that plan. He would happily settle for a few cupcake lovers coming by and maybe a handshake or two. And they would use the typing room for the arena. He figured his retirement was no big deal, and if he selected the other big show plan, he ran the risk of being the only one who showed up. He didn't want to stick his neck out and take any big risks. Every decent gambler knows when to hold them and when to fold them. And he certainly didn't want to be dragged in front of a huge crowd with total panic on his face and his brain in lockdown.

At mid-morning LP's siesta was interrupted by a phone call. He was surprised to hear the voice of Detective Hal Schaefer of the sheriff's department.

He said, "I got your message and wanted to call you before your retirement. First, thanks for all the details on Richards. Richards was on our radar before you called us. We were able to get the warrant and made the search of the store. We did find drugs on the premises. Richards also had several handguns, and one is the same caliber as the weapon used on Gonzales. A testing for a match is being done now. The status of the Gonzales murder had been going nowhere; this may give us a solution. Mr. Richards is now in the county jail. Thank you for your help on this. Good luck on your retirement."

LP thanked Schaefer for getting back to him on the raid. What a relief. LP had gotten lucky. He would have been a real goat if there were no drugs or guns in that store. Now it sounded like the case was closed.

Shortly before noon, nearly everyone in the office gathered in the small meeting room of the building. It was the perfect farewell party for LP, even though he had to say a few words before the group. LP mumbled a few incoherent words to those who had gathered before everyone adjourned to the cupcakes and cookies.

Also present at the gathering was the chief probation officer, who congratulated LP on his retirement and thanked him for his years of service to the department. LP was then presented with a plaque with his probation badge fused to it. His years of service were also inscribed on the plaque. LP would never get that badge off that board. It was attached there for eternity. You couldn't pry it off even if you tried forever. LP had hoped to waltz out of the building with that badge in his pocket and not on the plaque. You could always get into a lot of places with the old buzzer. Unfortunately it had to stay on that board. *Close but no cigar,* he thought.

As soon as the chief concluded his presentation to LP, one of the probation officers said, "Okay, LP, you aren't going to get off that easy. What do you plan to do after today? You must have something in mind. After all, you never shut up around here when we want a little peace and quiet. Get talking. What has been your philosophy to keep you going through all of your years here?"

LP thought for a moment before saying, "I guess my philosophy in one sentence might be, 'If you don't bite me, I won't bite you.' And a second guideline of life for me is borrowed from Jonathan Winters, the comedian, when he said, 'I'm just trying to me it to Friday.' It works."

Another officer said, "Good ones, LP. I may borrow them for the future. Now what about those future plans for you?"

LP smiled and said, "I'm not thinking that far ahead right now, but I know the first thing I plan to do. I'm going to load up my kayak on my car, throw in a few clothes, and head for Nevada. On the way I plan to stop at a lake or two and give each one a good paddling. I won't be in any big hurry to get where I'm going. In Reno I'm going to one of my favorite casinos. I will walk in the door and walk to the nearest roulette table. I usually never bet more than fifty cents on any roll of the wheel. But on this lucky day, I'll take a twenty-dollar bill from my wallet and place it straight up on one number, any number. One roll, all or nothing at all. The odds are thirty-five to one. If I win, I will have seven hundred dollars."

"But what if you lose, LP?" asked Dale Pierce.

"In that case, I'll skip dinner or just have a hot dog somewhere."

Someone else had another question. "But LP, what if you win?"

LP pondered for a moment and said, "In that case, I would let it ride. Seven hundred dollars times thirty-five comes to twenty-four thousand five hundred dollars. When I let it ride, actually I only have twenty dollars at risk. The house has twenty-four thousand five hundred dollars at risk. It seems like it's worth the risk. You aren't going to get very many chances to try that. If I lose on the second roll, I'll just skip dinner. I'm only out twenty dollars at the very worst. Do you think I'm being a little overly optimistic?"

Nobody said anything, but some chuckled while a few just looked skyward.

By this time, the cupcakes were reduced to crumbs, and LP's audience started to drift away to lunch or back to their regular tasks. The party was officially over. One of the last to leave the party was Shirley Luster, who said to LP, "We hope you didn't forget about our party. It's still on for this evening."

LP gave Shirley a big smile and said, "I've had it on my mind all week. I wouldn't miss it for anything. And this time my trunks aren't going to fall apart like last time."

"Oh heck, we were looking for an encore. You won't be able to top last week's fantastic performance. Oh well, that's life, I guess. We'll see you there."

After the chief probation officer handed LP the plaque with his badge stuck to it, it hit him that it was finally over. No turning back. The ball was now in his court. A new chapter of his life would start now. He had burned his bridges, and he had no new plan. He told himself, *This may be another fine mess you've got yourself into.* The only thing scheduled in his mind was to head east, young man. But who knows? There might be some cloudy skies in that direction. But tonight would be a warm evening with a full moon and a dip in the pool.

CHAPTER 23

When LP got home, he assembled the few things he would take with him for his trip out of town. By that time, it was late enough to head for the party at Shirley's. LP broke out his new swimsuit and put it on under his trousers. He wouldn't be dressed like a bum, and the new trunks would be safer than a chastity belt.

When he got to Shirley's place, he could hear the soft, light music coming from the backyard. He let himself in through the side gate. Last week he had expected a mob of people, but this time nobody was around except for Shirley. She was relaxing on one of the lounge chairs.

LP yelled, "Anyone home? Hi, Shirley, what's happening? Not even your pals are here tonight? Am I at the wrong house? Is my reputation driving people away?"

"No, you found the right house. I just don't know what happened to the girls. They were ordered to be here an hour ago. What do you think? Have we been set up by those two? Maybe they're just late."

LP responded, "LP is never set up. He just modifies. What you see is what you get. I want to break in my new swimsuit tonight, so you are stuck with me. May I sit?"

"Of course you can sit and help yourself to the 7UP. I hope you don't mind, but I'm having my usual."

"Not at all, drink hardy. I brought along a couple of my favorite CDs, but you don't have to listen to them if you prefer what you're playing now."

Shirley said, "No, I want to hear what you've got. The kind of music a person likes can tell a lot about the person. Did you know that?"

LP gave Shirley a big smile and said, "I just love your musical taste, Shirley, but now you've got me scared. Maybe I should put these CDs back in my car. I'm afraid to have my head shrunk. I don't know what might dribble out."

"LP, I promise I will not shrink your head. You are a very fine, well-balanced gentleman. Nothing but goodies will dribble out, I'm certain."

"I don't know about the gentleman part; you could be surprised. When your CD is finished, I'll put on something by Thomas Talbert entitled *Louisiana Suite*. It's jazz with lots of sweet sax. Or I can give you a little Floyd Cramer for some real good piano stuff. If you can't stand it, just scream."

After LP got settled in a lounge chair, Shirley said, "LP, I am a very curious person. Your name is LP. I'd be surprised if you said your parents gave you that name. What does LP stand for? I promise I won't tell a soul."

"It's no big secret. Actually, my name is Lawrence Patrick Cinch. When I was very young, they called me Lawrence or sometimes Larry. I hated both of those names. I hated Larry the most, and I got called that the most. Finally, after I griped enough, my relatives started calling me LP, and it stuck. In high school everybody called me LP. Most of the teachers called me Lawrence.

"Like all the other kids in a small high school, you had to go out for all sports or you wouldn't have a team. I went out for everything. We had some good teams because all the other towns were also quite small. I played pretty well. After a while, somebody came up with the gimmick that since LP Cinch was on the team, we would win because LP made it a lead pipe cinch. There was no Lawrence after that. It was now a lead pipe cinch. And the LP stuck with me after that. Actually, my paychecks have Lawrence on them, and they put Lawrence on that plaque they gave me yesterday. Otherwise I sign everything LP."

"Well, Mr. Lead Pipe Cinch," said Shirley, "that is a really rare twist. I promise I won't call you Lawrence, and I won't tell anybody about your real name. But I do think Larry is very cute."

They shared a couple drinks. Shirley drank scotch, and LP stuck with 7UP. They talked about their favorite music and musicians. Finally Shirley asked LP if he wanted to take a dip in the pool before it got too cool outside. LP agreed it was a good idea. She pulled off her shorts and blouse and was wearing another very small swimsuit. She looked great. She walked over to the pool and dove in. She looked up and said, "The water is great—nice and warm. Jump in."

LP stood by the pool and removed his shirt and pants. He was glad he was able to show off his new suit instead of any of his ancient ones. As he prepared to dive in, he was hit by one of his impulsive moments.

He said, "I've got no secrets around here anymore. At the last party, I revealed all. This evening no one will have the opportunity to tear my royal garments from me." He dropped his trunks to the ground and kicked them to one side. Once again he was as naked as a jay bird.

"This will be my final performance of the evening. Gratuities from the audience will gladly be accepted. Deposit your offerings at the front desk. All large bills will be gratefully accepted." With that LP dove into the pool and came up behind Shirley. He saw the exposed bikini string, but he kept his paws off it. He had escaped with his life the first time, but he didn't want to risk it again.

They paddled around in the water and talked for a while when suddenly Shirley made the remark, "I just remembered my mother called this morning and said she was going to bring some clothes of mine that she had to do some sewing on. She said she planned to drop them off this evening. That's this evening. You will love my mom."

With a look of terror on his face, LP said, "Your mom is coming sometime this evening?" Faster than a rocket, he swam to the pool exit and climbed from the water.

Shirley said, "LP, what are you doing? You are the craziest guy sometimes."

LP ran to his suit, began to put it on, and said, "I'm getting dressed before your mom shows up. Do you think I want her to see me running around naked? She'll think I'm some sort of pervert or worse."

Shirley laughed and said, "My mom probably won't even show up tonight. Anyway, she is a nurse. It wouldn't faze her."

"It would faze me big time. I'm glad you warned me. If she came when I was in the pool, I would have to stay in the pool until she left, and what if she decided to stick around? I'd look funny spending the entire night in the pool."

Earlier in the evening, LP had a few slightly, evil thoughts in his mind, but alas, none of the thoughts bore fruit. But it could have also been a disaster. What if Shirley's mom had dropped in? *Yes,* thought LP, *just another close but no cigar event. But there is always tomorrow.*

"Well, LP," said Shirley, "I guess we won't be seeing you after tonight. I assume you're leaving town tomorrow. Everybody is going to miss you. We hate to see you go."

"Yes," said LP. "Tomorrow I'm taking off. But I'm beginning to wonder if it's a good idea. Retiring is a very good plan, but leaving Two Rivers might be a bad deal. The thing is, I need to get away from everything for a bit. My mind is in a tizzy. However, I've lived in this town for a long time, and all of my friends are here. I don't know if I want to give all that up. You may get a local phone call from me one of these days asking if

I can go swimming with you. Or maybe you'd like to do a little kayaking. I've got an extra boat. Kayaking is easy and lots of fun. If I called, you wouldn't hang up on me, would you?"

"Of course not, LP. You can swim in my pool anytime, and I'd take you up on the kayaking."

"Well, I guess I better hit the road for now so I can get an early start tomorrow. I've absolutely enjoyed your big parties. Next time I see you, I hope it will be an official date. Okay?"

"Okay, Lawrence Patrick."

As they both walked to the gate, LP said, "Well, what about it?"

With a puzzled look, Shirley answered, "What about what?"

"What I told you before what I'd wished for. I told you I wanted to kiss a probation officer. How about it?"

Shirley smiled, and LP gave her a soft, gentle kiss.

LP sighed and said, "My dream has come true. Now let's make this a habit, babe."

Both laughed as LP leisurely strolled to his car, whistling as he went.

CHAPTER 24

Early Saturday morning, after LP got the basics loaded into his car, he decided to have a relaxed meal for a change, so he stopped at a place near his home and grabbed some bacon and eggs. As he munched away, he decided he wasn't going to second-guess himself on his recent decisions. He didn't have to come up with any grand plans in a day or in a week. Up to now he'd had a comfortable, livable lifestyle. Now it had changed. One major reason he had let the past go south was his dread of being transferred into adult or juvenile court. Now he was free of that concern. If he could invent a new job for himself, he would have tried something that made him his own boss. He realized those jobs had very little security. With a role like that, LP would be responsible for LP. He would have the responsibility of inventing that rare occupation. He knew that job was there somewhere. Perhaps it was back in Two Rivers. He decided to delay making any plan for at least one week. The following week would be one of loafing.

After a quick ascent into the mountains, LP came down from a high point, and below and in front of him laid Donner

Lake at fifty-eight hundred feet above sea level. Compared to Lake Tahoe, Donner was very small at about two and a half miles long and about half a mile wide. It looked like a precious jewel surrounded by high peaks and a forest of green. Usually in the early morning the water was calm, but as the day progressed, breezes often provided enjoyable paddling for boaters. This place was one of LP's favorites. The blue skies above added to the beauty.

Donner Lake's first claim to fame was the 1846 tragedy of the stranded Donner party, which became trapped near the lake in mountains covered with winter snow. Rescue parties were unable to rescue the people until later in the spring. Forty-seven starving people were rescued; however, eighty-nine people perished. Many had resorted to cannibalism to survive. During the winter, snow levels in the mountains normally reach as much as fifteen feet or more.

LP was anxious to proceed to Reno, so he cut his boating time down to several hours. He planned to return in the days ahead. He would spend more time at Lake Tahoe.

In Reno, LP parked his car in a public garage and would plan for somewhere to sleep later. His small suitcase with the swag would be safe for now in the trunk of his car. He had pledged to his fellow workers to do some crazy gambling. He couldn't fail to keep his word, so off he went to the casino.

Before he left his car, LP remembered a letter he had to mail. He took it and spotted a mailbox while he walked to the casino. He dropped the letter into the slot. It was going to three friends back home, and was from Big Al Jr. It would have a Reno postmark on it. Boy! Big Al sure does get around. That would take care of his pals for a month.

As planned, LP walked into the casino and gave his eyes a second to adjust a bit. He walked over to the nearest roulette table and took a twenty-dollar bill from his wallet.

He looked at all the thirty-six numbers on the green felt. What did it matter what number he selected? There was only one other player at the table. LP slapped the twenty on number nineteen, looked at the croupier, and said, "All of it on number nineteen."

The man nodded. LP slid into a chair at the table. In a few seconds, the ball was flying over the numbers as the wheel turned. It came to rest on number nineteen.

The customer next to LP yelled, "Wow, you had twenty bucks on that number."

LP said, "Yes. It's unbelievable. It will be about seven hundred dollars."

The croupier began sorting out stacks of chips to make LP's payoff.

LP interrupted, "Don't count it out. Let's just let it ride."

The amazed dealer looked up and said, "You want to let all of it ride?"

"Yes, let her ride. Let her flicker."

The croupier looked around him for the pit boss and signaled him. The pit boss walked over and said, "Yes?"

"This man wants his seven hundred dollars to ride on the next roll. He had twenty dollars on one number, and it came up."

Casinos have limits on maximum bets to protect themselves. The pit boss stood in thought for a pregnant moment and finally said, "Okay, let him make the bet." He knew the chance of hitting the same number twice in a row was almost impossible. The house would win their seven hundred dollars back in one roll of the wheel—a no-brainer.

By now a rather large group of customers had gathered around the table to watch the big roll. All eyes were glued to the roulette wheel. The man next to LP said, "Listen mister, I'm getting a couple chips on number nineteen too. I got to see this." He placed two twenty-five-cent chips on nineteen. The pit boss remained where he had stood. This was going to be an interesting spin, to say the least. His job might depend on the outcome.

The croupier spun the wheel and released the ball; the moment of truth for all.

Jack Mannion

At this point of the LP Cinch adventure, this author must interrupt. You, the reader, will not believe the result of the spin, not in a hundred years. Therefore, the author isn't going to reveal the result. Is it zero, or is it twenty-four thousand five hundred dollars? LP has admitted that in the past he has been untruthful; he has lied. He says all people lie—everybody, the author, even you. Therefore, none of us, including LP and the author, can actually be trusted to tell it as it happened. We will have to press on in the dark.

However, it is interesting to note that as LP arose after the big roll, planning to get an early dinner, a well-dressed man approached him. He introduced himself as an employee of the casino.

He said, "You created a great deal of excitement here this afternoon, and the casino would like you to have a room at our casino for the night, compliments of our club."

LP agreed to accept the generous offer. He thought, *How charitable the club has suddenly become. This has never happened before. Do you suppose the club doesn't want me to leave now? They don't ever pay you when you lose.* Maybe they were hoping if he remained in the club for the balance of the night, he might drop another twenty bucks in their place or maybe even more than twenty.

After LP got settled into his fine casino suite, he began to get quite hungry. Originally he had planned on a dinner of a hot dog and a soda at a casino lunch stand. As he thought about it, he decided that you only live once, and to celebrate his retirement, he would go for a nice prime rib dinner. And why not have it in the celebrity room of the casino? With the meal you got a little candlelight and music. Their prime rib dinners were rated the best in town. One thing he also decided was he would do no more gambling for the evening and maybe none for the entire trip. You had to watch those nickels and dimes. Money doesn't grow on trees. Tomorrow he would get up early and do a little shopping for coins. There were a lot of pawn shops in this town with a bargain or two.

That homeless money in the trunk of his car was doing nothing but gathering dust. LP decided he had to do something with part of it. He would take a small part of it—maybe about five thousand dollars—and buy a few US coins. Gold was currently well under four hundred dollars an ounce. That would mean he could buy a twenty-dollar gold piece in good condition for a little over four hundred dollars. In the past two years, gold had been twice that high. The price jumps all over the place, but over the years gold's value increases. When gold was discovered in California many years ago, the value of one ounce was twelve dollars. Currently it was thirty-five times that much. That's what you call inflation and distrust of paper money. LP knew that if he bought or sold gold at a coin store or a pawn shop and used cash, no would be questions asked. The transaction would only take a few minutes. LP would be looking for coins that were very close to the meltdown value. He wanted good, clean US coins, but not rare coins. Then he could let inflation give him a profit.

LP enjoyed a good night's sleep in his plush casino suite, but alas, the following morning he was back on the street, an orphan again. The casino owners must have been monitoring him and decided he wasn't gambling and was written off as a deadbeat. As a result, LP found a modest motel room about a mile away from the casinos. His choice was one of the many motels that lined the streets and were within walking distance of all the action. His choice had a nice swimming pool, and LP would make good use of it.

For the rest of the day and the following day, LP hit all the pawn shops and made short work of the five grand he had allocated for coins. He was pleased with his selections. The weight of his total purchases came to less than one pound. It was just pocket change and walking around money. It ended up in his car's trunk in short order.

For the next two days, LP spent much of his time in the motel pool. He also liked to walk around the casino and business areas, window shopping and observing the pedestrians buzzing here and there. He killed time in some bookstores and bought a couple books. He couldn't find a library, which was great for a man with no plan or time schedule. The slot machines all around him beckoned, but he resisted their call.

He wanted a change of scenery. The next day he would head south a few miles to Carson City, the small, historic capitol city of the state. Carson City actually had a US mint in years gone by when silver poured out of the ground. But those days had ended, and the mint building was now just another building on the main street. The city did have a couple pawn shops, and LP made several modest purchases while he was there.

After a night in Carson City, LP drove west toward the east shore of Lake Tahoe. Tahoe is a body of water named "big water" by its early inhabitants, the Washoe Indians. And it is big, being twenty-two miles long and twelve miles wide. Its deepest depth is over sixteen hundred feet. The lake is fed by snow-covered mountains, some with elevations of nearly nine thousand feet. The water of the lake is said to be 97 percent pure and as clear as glass. That's pure water.

When kayaking near the shore, a paddler can look down in the crystal clear water and clearly see large rocks and boulders that are probably twenty-five or thirty feet below. The surface is usually calm in the early morning hours, but later in the day, no sensible kayaker would be found anywhere but very near the shore. The breeze causes very large, threatening waves.

Today there was no wind, and the sun would be warm. As he crossed along toward Tahoe, he came upon a high point with a small roadside rest area, where he pulled over and parked. Below was a beautiful view of the lake. He enjoyed the sight, and at the same time, he thought back to what had happened a week earlier. There had been many changes. Since then, things had gone perfectly.

He looked up into his rearview mirror and said to his image, "It can't get any better than this. You have been on one big roll. A good roll."

There were times in the past when he'd felt close, but no cigar, but today he looked straight into the mirror and loudly proclaimed to himself, "Give that man a CEEGAR." He had rung that gong, and he wanted to keep ringing it.

He pulled out of the rest stop and headed for a spot on the lake called Zephyr Cove. He found a place to park his car and where he could put on his swimsuit. Within minutes he was flopping his boat into the water. It was warm out, and the wind was calm. This was what the trip was all about. He would hang around until he was good and tired. Then he would spend the night at South Lake Tahoe, a favorite place for gamblers, but there would be no gambling for him.

As he patrolled up and down the shoreline, he sorted out in his mind an upcoming plan for himself. After a few days of loafing, he was beginning to tire of this plan. And he was actually beginning to feel a little homesick. He had enjoyed these days, but that can only last so long. He hadn't talked to a soul he knew for days. He missed Two Rivers. He missed his friends and especially one young lady. There—he had arrived at a big decision. He was heading back to his old haunts in Two Rivers.

And what would he do when he got back there? He was beginning to make a few decisions on those issues too.

One of the books he bought at a Reno bookstore had lots of stuff that could be food for thought if you let it, and LP planned to let it do just that.

In the book he had read a quote by Thomas Merton, a twentieth-century *Trappist* monk and writer. Among other things, he wrote *The Seven Storey Mountain*. One of his quotes was, "Every moment and every event of every man's life on Earth plants something in his soul." This is pretty heady stuff if one believes one has a soul, and LP believed that quite a few people think they do. If so, one might want as many positive entries as possible to help negate the many negative marks that certainly transpire. LP could think of a long negative list that would show up on his record. He was enjoying himself, but he decided he had to get back to earth, do something constructive, and try a new direction with some positives in it. He wanted something he liked and something others would profit from.

After several hours of floating around in his dream world, LP dragged his kayak ashore and loaded up. He knew he would sleep well in South Lake Tahoe that night after this workout. He realized this journey was just what the doctor ordered. LP had cut through any confusing doubts about what he should do next. He had planned to stop at Donner Lake on his way back home, but he decided he wanted to get back to Twin Rivers as soon as possible. There was work to be done. He would need at least a full week or more to get his plan off the launching pad. He wouldn't even let anybody know he had returned until he had gotten his feet fully off the ground.

CHAPTER 25

For the next few days after his return, LP was busy creating a new LP world. He had to find a workplace and one that was in the middle of the city near the courthouse. His headquarters had to be simple and inexpensive. He needed business cards, a telephone, and a few pieces of furniture. After that, things would begin to take shape.

While these details were being completed, LP decided to finish one project out of his office that needed resolution one way or another. He needed to pay a visit to his three pals from a previous life and their dog. Early in the morning had always been a good time to find them at home, so he got an early start. When LP walked through the gate, Earle and Phil were smashing a few aluminum cans under their heels. They had apparently just returned from a can search.

Earle looked up and said, "It's Mr. Cinch. Hi, Mr. Cinch."

"Earle, I'm not Mr. Cinch anymore. I'm just LP or Cinch but not mister anybody. How have you good people been doing since I saw you last? Keeping out of trouble, I hope."

"Oh, we're doing real good, LP. How come you came to see us? Did you go back to work?"

"No, I'm still retired. I'm not here about any probation stuff. The reason I'm here is because Mr. Al Capone Jr. got a hold of me and said he wanted me to figure out a new deal for you three. He isn't dumping you or anything like that, but he said he hated doing all of this letter writing every month. He suggested that I help you three to start up some sort of business for yourselves. If you had money from your own business, he wouldn't have to send letters every month. He said he would give you some money to start the business and then you'd be on your own. He wanted me to talk to you about it and see what you think."

Earle looked a bit confused and said, "Gosh, we don't know what kind of business we could start. We've never had any real business. All we know what to do is what we've been doing."

LP nodded and said, "I know that, and Big Al knows that too. That's why he wants me to help you folks figure out something you would really like and something you could do real easy without any help. And you know what? I thought about one thing the three of you could be real good at. You are already almost experts at it now, you might say."

"What's that?"

"It's a lot like what you are doing now. Instead of picking up cans and crawling around in Dumpsters, why not open your own aluminum can depot? You buy cans from people around here, sell the cans to the state, and make a profit. The closest can depot around here is a couple miles away, isn't it?"

"Yes, it's over on Ford Street, and it's a long walk from here. But we don't have a truck or any of the things you need to run one of those places. We don't even have a place to run a depot."

"I know that, and I told Big Al about what you would need. I said you could only do this with quite a lot of money to get started. He said he knew that, and he would give you cash up front if he felt you could handle a business like that."

Earle was getting a little excited now and said, "Oh, it wouldn't be that hard if we had a place to do it and a truck to haul the cans to the big pickup place."

LP asked, "Does anybody here have a driver's license?"

"I've got one," Earle replied. "I have a license at the wrecking yard. Sometimes I go out with the wrecker to pick up cars and wrecks."

"That's great. I bet you work on cars enough over there to know how to keep a truck running."

"Oh sure. I'm an expert in that area."

"Good," said LP. "And I bet you could find a small truck or a pickup and trailer for under three thousand bucks. You'd need something that runs good, but it doesn't need to look pretty. If you had that, a good scale, and a few other items, you would be in business.

"I told Big Al about all that," said LP, "and I explained that you also had to have a couple thousand in cash to pay out when people come in with their cans, plastic, and glass. Al said he could come up with five grand and no more.

"One last and most important thing you need is a permit from the state to be in business. I will help you on that part of the deal. You four should easily be able to handle all the work involved in this business."

"All four?" replied Earle. "There are only three of us."

"You left out Biff. He can be your guard and night watchman."

"Well, we can't open a business here," said Barbara. "There's no room, and Leo, the grocer, wouldn't allow it if there was."

LP smiled and said, "I've tracked down the perfect place for a rental, and the price is very reasonable."

"You did?" said Earle. "Where is it?"

"It's right across the street from you guys. It's the abandoned gas station. It has a nice little office and a big lot around it. They've even removed the gas pumps, and there is a high security fence all around the property. I checked, and the rent is about two hundred a month. Why don't you folks talk it over and let me know if you want to take the big dive? If you do that and things work out, Al is going to stop the letters. No more money coming in the mail."

Earle said, "I don't know about Barbara and Phil, but I would sure like to do that. It would be easy with all of us in it together."

His partners both said they wanted to be in on the plan.

"Okay. I'll get back to Big Al and tell him your decision. If this goes through and people ask where you got the money, you can say you got an inheritance from a relative or you took out a loan. One big thing is you will have to keep good records and pay your bills every month. You would be the only outlet around here for miles. I think you would get a lot of business. Half the people around here collect those cans and plastic bottles."

LP figured that if he helped out in this venture, the little gang would be able to enjoy life pretty much as usual and improve their standard of living.

Later in the day, LP stopped at the local newspaper office and signed up for a small ad in the classified section of the per announcing he was now open for the business of "investigations and advice."

The following morning, LP had a fine breakfast at the Far West Coffee Shop about a block from his new work haunts. From there, he strolled back to his work desk and began working on the daily crossword puzzle in the local paper. Shortly thereafter he heard the office doorknob turn. LP had company.

"Hello, are you open for business?" asked an attractive, well-dressed lady as she stepped into the office.

"Yes, come in. How can I assist you?"

"I saw your business card on the bulletin board at the restaurant next to my store. I hope you can help me. Something terrible has happened, and I don't know where to turn. I'm just sick."

"Well, come in and sit down. Maybe I can help you out."

LP's guest seemed very rattled, nervous, and on the verge of tears. With a handkerchief at her eyes, she said, "Yesterday Alice was with me at my store. About noon she ran out the front door of the store and never came back. I looked all over and couldn't find her."

"You want me to help you find Alice?"

"Yes, we have to find her. I just don't know where to look or what to do. I'm just sick over this."

In a calming tone of voice, LP said, "Tell me about Alice. Who is she, and what does she look like?"

"I have a picture of her here in my purse. Let me get it." She fumbled briefly in her purse and handed LP a photo. "It's of Alice and me."

LP looked at the photo and saw a picture of his visitor holding a small, fuzzy dog with a pug nose. "This is a picture of you and your dog. Where's the one with Alice?"

"That's Alice I'm holding."

"Oh, I see. Alice is your dog, right?"

"She is not my dog. She is my sister's dog. My sister lives in Lakeview north of here, and I have been watching Alice while my sister and brother-in-law are visiting friends out of state. I have watched Alice lots of times before, but this is the first time she has run off. My sister will kill me if anything happens to her dog. I'm on the verge of a nervous breakdown over this. You've got to help me find her puppy."

LP thought, *I'll have to agree to help, big job that it isn't, or this lady is going to crumble right before my eyes. This wasn't in my plan.* He had to admit to himself that he had a long, close relationship with dogs, good and bad. He had never owned one and had been bitten by dogs on two occasions while working on the old job. *These animals just seem to be popping up in my life.*

LP said, "Okay now, cheer up and we will see what we can do. So yesterday the dog ran out of your store and never returned. Was the dog wearing a dog tag?"

"No. My sister lives in Lakeview, and the town is so small that they don't issue dog tags. She didn't even have a collar. This is a good picture of her. If you call her by name, she always wags her tail. My sister will be back in two days, and what will I tell her?"

"I'll tell you what," said LP. "I'm more accustomed to running down people, not animals, but I'll see what I can do. I'll work on this all day today. If I haven't had any luck finding the dog by then, I won't be able to give you any guarantees. My fee is usually fifty dollars a day. If I'm not successful, I'm not going to charge you anything. If I find Alice, you can pay me the regular rate. Give me your name, address at work, and phone number, and I will spend the day looking. I have several ideas."

"Oh, thank you," she said as she handed LP her business card. "I will be at the store all day. Call me right away if you have any luck. I am just frantic over this."

"Just relax. The dog will be found. I'll keep your picture for now and return it later."

After his client left, LP had to decide which destination would be first—the city or county dog pound. The city pound was closer, so he would try them first. If anyone found a dog without a tag, they most likely would call the pound. Otherwise an ad would show up in tomorrow's newspaper reporting a dog found and a reward requested.

When LP got to the pound, he explained he wished to see the latest crop of unfortunates. He was led to a room where a dozen dogs were caged. As he walked down the line, he spotted his little lost friend, Alice. To make certain, he looked at the dog and said, "Hi, Peppie. Here, Peepie." Nothing happened; the dog just gazed at him. Then he said, "Hi, Alice," several times. The pup began wagging her tail and became very active in the cage.

LP explained to the caretaker that he knew the owner of the dog, who would pick up the dog as soon as she was informed. He gave the caretaker the name of his client and asked what charges would be levied to get the dog released. The man said the dog had to have a tag and several shots. The cost would be about thirty dollars.

LP retreated downtown to the dress shop and explained everything to his client. With the good news, his client became a changed person. She was all smiles and said she would close the store immediately and rescue Alice. She said, "Thank you, thank you. I want to give you something in addition to your fee. Is there something here in the store you would like to pick out for your wife?"

"Well, right now I'm not attached, but I do know of someone who could always use another swimsuit. Do you have anything like that here? Maybe a bikini?"

"We have a large selection of the latest bikinis. Allow me to choose something very fitting. What size would you need?"

"Well, I don't know exactly. I think my friend could be about the same size as you, Mrs. Forest."

She smiled and said, "I'm also presently unattached, so you can call me Miss Forest or just Kay, if you prefer."

LP looked Kay up and down briefly, enjoying the view, and then stepped to one side to get a further peek.

LP nodded his head and said, "Well, Kay, as far as I can tell, you and my friend are exactly the same size. You could be twin sisters."

Kay smiled and said, "Let me pick something very nice, and I can gift wrap it for you. I can personally drop it off at your office tomorrow morning, but today I want to go get Alice before something happens to her. I won't let her out of my sight after this."

As LP headed for the door, he said, "Thank you very much. This is very generous and thoughtful of you, Kay. It was a pleasure solving the Alice case. You made my day."

As LP returned to his office, he realized that Alice might not be the only lucky dog today. Kay seemed to have been a bit chummy and was possibly looking to extend things a little further. LP smiled to himself and thought, *Oh, LP, you vain, egotistical brute, you. Always the dreamer.* Kay probably had only one dog on her mind, and that one was waiting for her at the dog pound.

In any event, he figured he was now one for one at his new job, as simple as the case was, and he had picked up a neat fifty dollar bill for an hour's work.

CHAPTER 26

Two days later but right on schedule, LP decided it was time to come out of the shadows. He would start with a phone call to Shirley at work. Eight thirty a.m. was usually a good time to catch a PO at work in the office.

When Shirley answered, LP said, "Hello, Shirley Luster. This is LP Cinch, the ex-probation officer. I'm calling because I need help. My uncontrollable urge to kiss a probation officer has returned, and I wondered if you could resolve this wonderful problem. And in case anyone wanted to know if I am still alive, I am."

"Well hello, Mr. Lawrence Cinch. We thought you were gone forever. It is good to hear you have returned to your old haunts. I assume you're back in our town. And it sounds like you are still full of malarkey. Nothing has changed since you left. It never changes. I'll ask around and see if any of the guys wants a kiss from you."

"Well, I enjoyed my brief recess, but I have now embarked on a new scam. I was hoping I could show you around at my new setup here in town. My operation is downtown on King

Street. I'm open for business every weekday. Maybe you'd let me take you to lunch after I show you around."

"The lunch thing sounds good to me. Name the day."

"What about this noon? The monkey has the day off, so he won't be a pest."

"Sounds good. Where is this place? Not the zoo, I hope."

"The address is one thousand and two King Street. It's the ancient ten-story building on the corner of Olive and King Streets. I'm on the third floor, office number thirty-two. You take the elevator. There is a parking garage just a block away on Olive and Swift Streets."

Shirley used the parking garage and walked the block to the old stone building on busy King Street. Many downtown workers were racing about to squeeze in their lunch hour, no doubt.

When she pulled open the heavy metal door to the building, she noticed the directory on the wall. On the listing she saw "Cinch and Mac," third floor, room thirty-two. The lobby, like the building itself, was ancient. It was all stone and marble with a very high ceiling and was dimly lit. The elevator also moved very slowly, as if it was tired.

LP's office was close to the elevator. On the glass door were the names LP Cinch and GT Mac. Under their names was "Investigations and Advice." *Very impressive*, thought Shirley. *He even has a partner.* She rapped on the window and opened the door at the same time.

There sat LP with his feet up on a large wooden desk, tilted back in his chair, reading a newspaper. The office was smaller than tiny. It had a large window at LP's back. You could view the city and get a suntan all at once. The only other things on the desk besides his feet were a telephone, an old-looking typewriter, and a cigar box. In a corner near the desk was a bulb-shaped, glass gumball machine with "1¢" inscribed on the glass. Otherwise the only other things in the room were two folding chairs and a small, slightly used-looking sofa. Very cozy indeed.

LP quickly folded his newspaper and slid it into a desk drawer. "Well, what do you think? Wild, isn't it? I've only been here for a short while and already I feel like Humphrey Bogart in *The Maltese Falcon.*"

Shirley said, "What do you do if you want to breathe?"

LP defensively replied, "Come on. What are you talking about? We got luxury here." Pointing out two interior doors, he added, "We have a fine restroom and a jumbo closet for files and my hat, if I buy one. What more could a successful working man need?"

Shirley looked back at the office door and asked, "I see you have a partner, a Mr. GT Mac. Where does he sit? In your lap?"

"Oh. There is no GT Mac. I just made him up. I think it looks more successful and official if you have more than one person running a business. And if something goes wrong, I can always blame Mac for messing up. There is just me and no GT Mac. Actually that name on the door is just an abbreviation of GTMAC, Give that Man a Cigar. It's a term I keep coming up with when things are just great. No, I am the boss, and I am the only employee. I give the orders, and I take the orders—just the way I love it. I'm going to work myself to death."

"Your door sign says 'Investigations and Advice.' What on earth does that mean? What kind of investigations?"

"Well, I'm trying to be a kind of jack-of-all-trades guy, I guess. I hope to do whatever I can legally do for whoever comes in the door. I don't have a private-eye license or any other kind of license. I don't have a permit to carry a gun. I will explain that to whoever might stumble in with a problem. If I can't help them, I'll tell them to look elsewhere. Otherwise I might help find a lost person, snoop on a cheating husband, or give cheap advice on anything I might have a handle on. I am spreading the word that I can serve court subpoenas and the like.

"I am also beginning to develop a charitable trust type of thing where the trust can give financial aid to needy children or young adults toward furthering their education. It'll do things like helping with tuition and textbook costs and things of that nature.

"I've already found one student who is very bright and has been in junior college but can't afford the costs of attending state college toward getting a degree. She happens to be a sister of one of the people I had on my probation caseload. She has had straight As all the way from first grade through a year of junior college. She wants to be a teacher, but her part-time job won't cover the cost of the state college tuition. My funds are somewhat limited now, but I hope to get voluntary donations from some prospective sources. This is going to be nonprofit, and no one will be accountable to anybody but me and the one getting the aid.

"Actually, I think I have a better part-time job for this student than the one she has now. I talked to Hy Mandel at juvenile hall about hiring her on as a temporary worker in the hall. They hire a lot of temporary workers. She could work there on the night shift and do her studying while the juveniles are sleeping. She'd get in a lot of hours and make more money than now. Maybe later on she might decide to become a probation officer like half of the people they have in the department now. Anyway, I put in a pitch for her if she wants to try it.

"The way we—meaning me—will handle any grant money is simple. I will give the person some money, and the recipient will bring back receipts. If more money is needed and there are funds available, the recipient will get more money. I will see the recipients on a regular basis and review grades and feedback. This is in the trial stage. I figure we could provide about three or four thousand bucks a year total. We would probably look at two recipients at a time for now. We will be looking for kids from down the river, poor kids, and farm kids who have demonstrated their dedication and need. Hopefully we could grow as we can show possible donors what we can achieve.

"The young lady I am working with is Maria Gonzales. I think she's a winner. Her talents won't go to waste."

Shirley shook her head. "LP, you are a genius. Where do you come up with all these ideas?"

"Well, I have connections—guys like GT Mac and others."

Shirley gave the room a closer inspection and noticed a mysterious, strange-looking framed item on the wall. She got up and examined it more closely. "What in the dickens is this thing? Tell me—what is it?"

"You should be very familiar with that famous souvenir. It was a star at a party you and I attended several weeks ago. Take a close look. You know it well. That is the swimsuit I was wearing on the night you turned me into a naked, quivering man. I had it flattened out and framed to remind me how people will do almost anything to see my Atlas-like naked body. The day will come when it will be world famous. People will come from near and far to view it."

"LP, you are the limit. Where do you come up with all this? And by the way, how did you find this office? It is one of a kind, although I must say it does have a Sam Spade atmosphere. After a while it could grow on you a bit—even attract some customers maybe."

"Years ago I took a stock market class at a local college. The teacher was a stock broker. You could actually buy stocks through him. He had his own one-man brokerage business. He was kind of a weird fellow. They called him Five-Share Franklin. He was a rebel. His office was in this very building. It was up on the tenth floor, and his office was smaller than my office, if you can believe that. All he had in his office was a desk like mine. He had a telephone and a copy of the daily *Wall Street Journal*, and that was about it. He encouraged beginning investors to just buy five shares of a stock at a time when they first got into the market. At that time, buying stock was pretty expensive, but if you bought five shares, the brokerage was livable. That's how he got the handle of Five-Share Franklin from other brokers. They would rather sell you one hundred shares and make more money. After you bought your five shares and wanted to buy more, he would encourage you to buy some other stock. That way you would end up with a more-balanced portfolio. That would tend to limit your risk to some degree. Just keep adding stocks, and pretty quick you have a nice-looking, balanced group of companies. I used to buy from him, and he put me into a lot of good stocks. He discouraged me on one stock called Taco Bell, though. Later it became part of a huge, successful company. You win some and you lose some.

"Anyway, I just loved the simplicity of his office and his business, so when I needed an office, I thought of this place first. The rent is unbelievably cheap for the location. I can sit here and look out at the people walking up and down the busy street. I get a free show regularly. I can take a city bus to and from work if I don't want to pay for parking.

"I finally have a job where I have no boss except me. That could be a huge step down. All orders come from me to me. No miscommunications possible. And I hope I don't turn out to be a nutty supervisor. In any other job, you are at the mercy of your boss. That's fine if they are good but bad if they have a screw loose. It's like something I learned when I first entered the army as a dumb, young lad. As a private, you just turn in your brain. It's not needed or wanted. Just follow orders. There are layers and layers of brains all up the chain of command doing your thinking for you."

"LP, I think you're a bit overboard on bosses and supervisors in any kind of business, public or private. Somebody has to give orders and assume responsibility or you just run around in circles and accomplish nothing."

"True, but let me give you an example of the other extreme that happens now and then. Sometimes it can result in some genuine humor and also not much sense. I had just been drafted into the army. Along with a train full of other recruits, I was being transferred from Chicago to a training camp in Missouri. Along the way, we had to be fed, and a sack lunch was the meal of the day. In all, there were five cars of hungry trainees.

"A big sergeant walked through the cars and ordered us not to throw anything out of the windows after we ate. He

183

explained that all paper and leftovers would be collected by several assigned recruits. The sergeant implied that anyone who didn't do it his way would be court-martialed. After the lunch, another recruit and I were selected to be the cleanup squad. The sarge told us to each take a thirty-gallon garbage can and walk through the train cars, retrieving every scrap of debris—a very simple task.

"When we completed the collecting, the sergeant instructed us to follow him to the last car of the train and from there to the platform of that car. I assumed we would leave the two cans on the platform to be emptied later. I figured this was the most adult and responsible thing to do with the garbage. I thought that was good thinking on the part of the army and the sergeant. Instead, the sergeant ordered us to dump the cans off the end of the speeding train. We did as ordered, and the countryside immediately looked like the inside of a chicken-plucking factory. Paper flew all over the fields on both sides of the train. I couldn't believe the logic of such an act. Farmers out in the middle of Iowa would be chasing down paper for a week or longer. After I saw that, I was surprised that the sergeant hadn't told us to throw the cans overboard also. You have to commend the sergeant for getting that part right. With all that criticism, I guess I have to point out that I never made the rank of sergeant while in the army.

"Now I've blabbed enough. Let's go get some lunch. They have a soup and salad place right around the corner, or there's always McDonald's if your time is limited. I was hoping you would let me take you out for dinner this evening to celebrate the return of LP Cinch. I promise it will be a decent restaurant."

"That would be nice, LP. We do have to have some sort of celebration in honor of your return and the start of a very interesting and unique business venture. I know it will be a success."

As they left LP's new headquarters and walked to lunch, LP stopped briefly at a post office box and dropped a letter in the slot.

He said, "It's just a brief note to three of my old friends. They have an excellent plan to open a new business. I may be able to give them a hand."

After lunch they parted, and LP headed back to his new office. *You never know when someone might need a little private eye work done*, he thought. Hopefully the ad he was running in the newspaper would stir up a little action, and he would his phone number in the telephone book later. These things would help. Otherwise he would remain an unknown soldier sitting in an unknown office. He wanted enough adventure coming in to require him to have to find a real live GT Mac to share the wealth.

The entire day wouldn't be wasted. He had the dinner date with Shirley later and had to remember to present her with the swimsuit he'd gotten her. He'd tell her he saw it in a store window and had to get it because it was made for her.

No sooner did LP get his face back in the newspaper than he heard his doorknob turn, and in walked a potential customer.

The big man who walked in was wearing a business suit with a fedora. "Hello. Is this where I can find Gregory Mac? Your ad in the newspaper had the name GT Mac in it. I had a buddy in the army named Gregory Mac. I haven't seen him since then and thought I better look him up. Is he around today?"

LP replied, "No, and he won't be around for a long time—actually never. I'm sorry to tell you there is no GT Mac here. I just put the name in the ad to give my operation a little more substance. When I used the name, I thought there couldn't be another person in the world with that name. Sorry to give you a bum steer."

"No problem," said the man. "I just came down here from Portland. I got tired of the weather up there. I thought Greg Mac could line me up with a little work. I have a private investigator license in the state of Oregon and have applied for one in California."

LP thought momentarily and then said, "Sit down if you have a minute or two. Let me tell you what's going on around here. I just retired after being a probation officer for years. I am just in the process of starting this business. I have no PI license, but there are some things I could do without a license. There also will be a lot of things I will have to pass up because I don't have a license. While you are looking for work, I could give anything that comes in here that I couldn't handle. I can't guarantee any steady work now, but it might help you some."

He said, "I could take a shot at that."

"Okay," said LP. "I don't even know your name. Can I see your Oregon license and your driver's license and get a little more information, like where you are staying and your phone number?"

The man produced his ID and said, "I'm Phillip Colt. Everybody calls me Phil. I've got an apartment a couple blocks from here. It's just a place to hang my hat for now. I checked a couple agencies and haven't had anything there so far. Your offer sounds good. I'm flexible on the pay. I just want to get back to work. I've got all the needed gadgets—the cameras and whatnot. And I've lived down here briefly in the past, so I know my way around town pretty good."

"Great," said LP. "Who knows? If all goes well, I'm sure I'll need a permanent partner. I could change my name to Winchester, and we could call the business 'Winchester and Colt Investigation.' Who could possibly ignore us with a handle like that?"

Phil laughed and said, "We would certainly get a lot of bites just on the name alone."

LP said, "Keep in touch, and drop in anytime. I have a cribbage board, or we could play a little rummy if things are slow."

The two shook hands, and while Mr. Colt was putting on his impressive fedora hat, he said, "I have a feeling this could work out real good."

After Colt left, LP gazed at the street below from his large office window. The foot traffic was heavy. Surely there had to be a few people out there who had a problem he could solve. He had to agree with what Phil had said: this could work out real good. He had a feeling it was just what the doctor ordered. A one-man act wasn't going to work. There would always be a need for backup. Sadly, he realized that his current shoebox office might have to be sacrificed. However, there were larger offices in the same building, and he wouldn't sacrifice the location; it was perfect.

LP thought about Phil Colt. One thing that had impressed him was Colt's hat. It made him look official in some way, like he was serious about what he was doing. LP decided to lock things up for the day and buy a hat just like Phil's. He would have to get a couple of his double-breasted suits out of the closet and into the cleaners. He was going to have to shed the T-shirts and Levis if he wanted to appear serious about this business. It would be back to neckties and white shirts. He hated the thought of going back to the structure of the past, but he had to reinvent himself a bit to fit the scene.

The following morning, LP reported to work without the fedora and double-breasted suit. However, he surrendered to a white shirt and necktie. He had decided to give himself time to adjust to his return to formal structure. He felt this was a step in the right direction.

As he briefly scanned the newspaper, he decided he was in the mood for a good cup of coffee. The instant stuff in lukewarm water was just not cutting it this morning. He taped a ten-minute sign on the office door, grabbed his newspaper, and headed to a nearby coffee shop for a coffee break.

On his return to his headquarters, he walked past a towering, historic church in the middle of the city. At the top of the church's concrete steps stood Father Mulligan, a longtime acquaintance of LP's.

As he walked up the steps, he said, "Well hello, Father Mulligan. What do you know? What do you say?"

Father Mulligan smiled and replied, "Hello, LP. How are you these days?"

"Things couldn't be better, Father. I hope it has been likewise for you."

Father Mulligan shook his head slowly and said, "It is a sad day today, LP. A real sad day."

"What could be that bad, Father?"

"Oh, it's my fault, I guess. Earlier after mass, at one of the side altars, I left a communion chalice out on the altar. When I came back to put it away, it was gone. I couldn't find it anywhere. Somebody took it."

LP nodded, "Oh, that is serious. It could be anyone. You don't lock up the church during the day. The public can come and go as they please. And I suppose you have steady streams of traffic coming to your residence for help or handouts all day long. This area is well populated with panhandlers and all kinds of people. Someone could have seen the chalice and stuck it under his coat and gone-o."

"Yes," said Father, "I guess that's what happened. Someone in desperate need, no doubt. The loss is not that great, but the chalice is a religious object and something that should not be desecrated. It needs to be back here in the church, but that's probably impossible. If somebody stole it, why would he return it? It's gone forever, and it's my fault."

LP pondered a moment and replied, "Don't write it off, Father. It may turn up. As we both know, you get a lot of bums and desperate people in this neighborhood, and one very large hobo hangout for the homeless is very close by, within walking distance."

"Yes, I know. We have our soup kitchen over there. We feed a lot of people over there every day of the year."

"Father, let me look into this. We might be able to pull off a miracle here, especially if you get going on your rosary and ask for some help from you-know-who. Let me try something before you report this to the cops, and I'll get back to you if my plan doesn't work."

LP assumed that no normal-minded person would steal something like a gold communion chalice. What could anyone do with it? It would be hard to sell it to anyone. No pawn shop would buy it. Any bum walking around trying to get money for a thing like that would alert the police in short order. What on earth would a buyer do with something like that? It would just mean trouble for anyone who had it in his or her possession.

LP asked, "Father, what time do they start handing out the next meal over at your soup kitchen?"

"They usually start serving at eleven thirty a.m."

"This is a long shot," said LP, "but with luck we might be able to scare that thing up before the sun goes down. I'll get back to you by then or sooner."

The time was 10:30 a.m. There would be a long line of hungry people in front of the soup kitchen very shortly, and LP would be there to try a little plan.

When LP arrived at the soup kitchen, approximately thirty hungry and weary-looking individuals were lined up outside the building awaiting their food. He had no idea how many people would show up, but he knew there were many more to come. As he slowly walked up close to the group, he thought about how fortunate he was. With just a few lifetime distractions, this could have easily been him in line waiting to be fed. This was possibly the highlight of these people's day.

In a loud voice, he asked for their attention. "I am LP Cinch, and I'm helping Father Mulligan. Father Mulligan is responsible for begging and pleading to local citizens and store owners for funds and food to keep this kitchen in business. He gets nothing for his many efforts. He works at this every day of the year. Today I was saddened to find out that someone removed a gold chalice from his church. They ripped him off. He was going to report it to the police, but I encouraged him to wait on that until I made an effort to get it back. Whoever took it can't do much of anything with it. The crook couldn't pawn it or sell it to anyone because the only person who would own such an item would have to be wearing a black suit and a Roman collar. Any other person would be broadcasting he had stolen it. Therefore, the thief who did this will get nothing for it except for a lot of big trouble. Most people would know better than to swipe something like that. That was a real stupid act. I figure that the culprit very likely lives down in the campgrounds with most of you folks. He probably already tried to sell it to one of you.

"If I don't get my hands on it in the next couple of hours, Father Mulligan will report it to the cops. Do you know what will happen then? Well, I'll tell you what. The cops will sweep into your fancy sleeping grounds—your home—and tear everything apart until they find that cup. They may take a few of you fellows back to jail in their search.

"If that chalice isn't in my hands today by one o'clock p.m.— that's an hour after noon—the cops will pay you an angry visit. My advice is that one of you, or several of you, find it and get it to me. The person who brings it to me will get three nice, crisp ten-dollar bills."

LP took three bills out of his shirt pocket and waved the money back and forth for all to see.

"No questions will be asked of the finder, and he will be a bit richer for his honorable deed. And to top that, the cops will know nothing about the theft.

"While I'm on the soapbox, let me give you a little religion for free. Remember Judas sold out Jesus for thirty pieces of silver. Somebody can make thirty dollars by making things right with Father Mulligan and God. The thief who stole this doesn't deserve a nickel. And if the chalice doesn't get into my hands by one o'clock p.m., you will all suffer when the cops start throwing all of your belongings all over the ground.

"I plan to sit on that bench on the riverbank where the two rivers come together, but one o'clock p.m. is the deadline. Pass the word around. I'll repeat this message a little later when everybody gets in the chow hall so everybody knows the scoop. After that you are on your own. I wouldn't let one creep screw up your life any more than it already is. And if anybody throws that chalice in the river or something like that, I swear I'll find out about it and will be extremely upset."

LP went to his car, which was nearby, and retrieved a can of Pepsi and the daily newspaper. From there he walked to riverside bench and began his wait. After enjoying his soda, he returned to the chow hall and repeated his message to a much-larger group of hungry customers. He spared them from his earlier biblical message about Judas. Prior to the meal, they had most likely gotten a few words along those lines from the management. After that he returned to his park bench and continued his vigil. He could give the newspaper his undivided and complete attention. However, he reviewed his plan again. He hoped he had not pulled a boner when he assumed the thief was in the group of unfortunates he had challenged. He realized he was very fortunate to get away with throwing his weight around with a bunch of very defeated people. Many of them might have disliked his little message. A lot of them looked like they could very easily have handed him his head. Maybe they decided it wasn't worth losing their place in the chow line. LP was amazed at how lucky he often was. Hopefully this was one of those times.

At 1:00 p.m. a rough-looking, bearded man walked up to LP at the park bench. Was this going to be one of those lucky times? LP watched as the man reached into a sack he was carrying. He said, "Is this the chalice you were looking for?" He pulled the object out and held it up.

"Bingo," said LP. "Oh, happy days are here again. Thank you, thank you. That's got to be it. I hope you didn't have a lot of trouble getting it back to me."

"No. It wasn't difficult. I had a couple of my friends help me out. We persuaded the guy that he should move on. He's planning to leave our camp today. We didn't want to see Father Mulligan getting ripped off like that. That was a real bummer."

LP reached in his pocket and pulled out the three promised ten-dollar bills. After handing them over, he pulled out his wallet and got two additional twenty-dollar bills. "You more than earned this. Keep it all, or share with your friends. It's up to you what you decide. You are making Father Mulligan a happy man. His prayers have been answered. Can I give him your name?"

"They call me Swede. I think Father knows me."

"Listen, Swede," said LP, "right now I am in a hurry to get this thing back to Father as fast as I can, but I want to give you my card with my address and my phone number. I don't know anything about you or your plans, but if you want to contact me sometime to chew the fat, this is where I am. I may not be able to help you in any way, but you never know. I'm a pretty good listener."

Swede took the card, gave LP a sharp salute, and walked back toward the campground.

A short time later, LP contacted Father Mulligan and returned the chalice. The priest was overjoyed, and he said he had been praying all morning. He kept thanking LP repeatedly.

"I did very little," said LP. "The one who did all the work was Swede. You know him. Thank him. He took care of all the details.

"Father, there is one thing you can do for me. Let me give you one of my business cards. In the future, if you run into people with some unusual problem or task who don't know where to go, give them my number. If I can help, my rates will be reasonable."

As LP walked back to his office, he realized he had walked on water again. But he also acknowledged to himself that water can also be ice, and you can't walk on thin ice, so he shouldn't get a big head. He could be in for a fall. Today he had recovered a stolen item. The other day he had rescued a lost dog. Both were noble achievements, but he had to drum up a lot more business than that to keep a little bread on the table.

At his office door, he removed his "back in ten minutes" note. Nobody had left any cards or messages at his door. He hadn't been missed. When he got to his desk, he removed a notebook from the drawer. In it he recorded the seventy-dollar reward money he had spent. That amount would be coming out of Margareta's sack of money. The list of disbursements was growing. LP would be recording every cent spent from the money bag. He didn't want one penny to go to himself. In the future, if he had to face the long arm of the law on the money issue, he could at least show that everything went to others for their betterment and not his. In a court trial, if LP had a smart lawyer and a sympathetic jury, a district attorney would really have his work cut out for him.

LP decided he'd had enough exciting adventure for one day and gave himself the rest of the day off. Since he wanted to be a good boss, he couldn't be a slave driver all the time. He knew he had to give the hired help a little consideration once in a while if he wanted a smooth-running operation. LP needed a little free time anyway to get ready for the swimming party he was going to later in the evening.

CHAPTER 27

Phil Colt shuffled the cards briefly, slapped them on the desktop, and said, "Cut the cards."

LP and Phil were engaged in a game of cribbage in LP's office after a three-day job of serving a batch of summons for the local court system. When LP was offered the job, he had grabbed it and called Phil to offer him part of the action. Phil agreed.

"Well, we did get the job finished," said Phil, "but I never knew how hard it would be to run down all those people for what we will be paid. It's better than nothing, I guess. I suppose that beggars can't be choosers, but if something doesn't happen around here pretty quickly, I many have to head back to rainy Portland for something to do."

The card game continued in silence briefly before the telephone rang. Phil smiled and said, "If that's a call offering more work serving up summons, tell them I just left town for Alaska."

LP replied, "Okay, and I'm your chauffer."

They both smiled as LP said into the phone, "Cinch and Colt. How can I help you?"

After listening to the caller for a brief time, LP pulled a tablet in front of him and began taking notes. He said, "Mrs. Troutman, we would be glad to assist you in this serious matter. You definitely called the right place. We will be here in the office during the noon hour if you plan to come in, but let me get a few more details now, if you don't mind. First, what's your husband's name, and where does he work?"

As he took further notes, he said, "It would be very helpful if you could provide us with a photo of your husband, and in a case like this, we will probably need three or more days to give you all the needed information. This could probably only be done with two or more operatives involved. We can discuss rates when you come in. I think you will find that we are very reasonable and professional. I will personally be involved in the matter, along with my best agent, if he is free at the time. Hold on. Let me speak to him right now."

LP held his hand over the phone to ask Phil if he wanted in on the case. "The wife thinks her husband is wandering off the ranch, maybe has a girlfriend on the side. It sounds pretty simple, and she sounds desperate enough to come with some pretty good cash."

Phil said, "Great, count me in. This is just my line, and I welcome it."

LP continued his phone conversation. "My partner, Mr. Colt, is available and will assist me. Your husband will have no suspicions that he is being investigated. We await your noontime visit."

As he hung up, LP explained, "Mrs. Beverly Troutman thinks her husband is stepping out on her. She says he often works late and doesn't get home until quite late in the evening. Several times she has attempted to telephone him on late nights at work, and nobody answers the phone. She said he likes to play cards and gamble a bit, but she doesn't think gambling is an issue. She fears it is another woman. She related that he recently got some angry phone calls at home, but he told her it was just someone at work who is a bit of a mental case and she shouldn't worry about it.

"She is coming in during the noon hour, so why don't you stick around and we will get more details? He works just up the street as a bookkeeper. She is a dental assistant and works downtown near here. She said he usually parks his car in the city parking lot just up the street. His car is a grey Ford pickup, about a 1979 model with a small camper on the back. She said the license plate number ends with two hundred twenty-two and starts with eighteen. She can't remember the middle numbers. It will be an hour and a half before she shows up. Why don't you walk over to the parking lot now and scout around in there to see if you can spot that pickup? Meanwhile I'll check out where he works. It's only two blocks away. We can get back to our card game later. This woman sounds very anxious and willing to agree to a pretty good-sized quote from us. I'll give her a high one. I'm getting tired of all this charity work. We got to make hay while the sun shines."

"That sounds good to me," said Phil. "No more free lunches from us for a change. I doubt she wants to put this off. She wants answers right now. Money is no object."

Phil got up and headed for the door as he placed his fedora firmly on his head. LP realized Phil wasn't as tall as he originally appeared to be. That hat added an inch or more. And he also wore western boots, adding an additional inch or more in height. LP reasoned that in this business, it didn't hurt to look a little taller than the next guy.

A short time later, the two shared their findings. Phil reported, "The pickup is parked on the ground floor of the lot. It has a small camper on the back, and the license number is 2227918. The hood of the pickup is covered with paint primer, and it's a pretty beat-up looking thing. There's nothing unusual about it."

LP said, "Troutman works on the third floor of the building. There appears to be about three dozen people working in the place. Everybody uses an elevator from the large lobby to come and go, so our man will be using that front door to get in and out. He won't be able to sneak off on us."

Shortly after noon, Mrs. Troutman stepped into LP's office. She was fashionably dressed, very attractive, and probably in her late thirties. She said, "I'm Mrs. Troutman, and I don't have to be back at work until one thirty p.m."

LP introduced himself and told her Phil was the person who would be involved. Mrs. Troutman repeated much of what had been covered earlier. She made note of the fact that her husband could not be aware of any of this. She said, "I hope there is a simple, positive answer to all of this. I don't know if my husband is in danger or if our marriage is in danger, but I have to know what's going on."

"We can begin our work today as your husband leaves work," said LP as he handed her a summary of the costs, "and we request payment for the first day in advance."

She examined the paper briefly and said, "I don't want my husband to see this charge in our checkbook. I will pay cash for all billing."

"Very good," said LP as he glanced at Phil with a look of relief. He had highballed her, and she took it without blinking an eye.

As he took the remittance from her, he added, "I think it's best if we contact each other by telephone at your workplace. Otherwise you can call in here or just come in anytime. Is your pickup your only car?"

"No. I drive a Ford Mustang. We use the pickup for camping or whatever."

"Were you able to bring a photo of your husband?" asked LP.

"Oh yes. I almost forgot to give it to you." As she handed the photo to LP, she noted, "This was taken of us at a campground last summer."

It was a good shot of Mrs. Troutman and her husband in the woods in front of a tent. *This photo should work fine,* LP thought, and he asked if he could keep it for a while. He passed it to Phil.

197

"By all means," said Mrs. Troutman. "Call me early at work tomorrow to let me know how it is proceeding. Now I must get back to work."

After Mrs. Troutman left, LP and Phil got back to another card game. LP said, "Troutman gets off work around five o'clock p.m. You can hang around the front of his office building and follow him. In the meantime, I'll park my car outside the parking lot gate and follow him in my car if he decides to drive his car somewhere, maybe home or maybe to a tryst. Either way, I'll see you here tomorrow. If he goes home, I'll do the same, and we'll run the drill again tomorrow."

Shortly after 5:00 p.m., Phil spotted his man leaving the building and walking up the street toward the parking lot. However, the man proceeded on for another block and walked into a public card room. After lingering on the street for several minutes, Phil decided to go into the place like a customer. When he entered, he walked over to a lunch counter next to a number of card tables, most of which were occupied by gamblers. He ordered a beer and casually scanned the room; his man had already occupied a space at a nearby table.

Phil nursed the beer for about twenty minutes and observed his man. Troutman didn't appear to be that involved. On each hand he anteed and then folded his cards before the hand was over. He looked like a real loser. Maybe he was distracted or something. In very short order, he got up and made for the exit. Phil followed soon after. His man made straight for the parking lot and headed for his car. Phil noted LP's car parked near the entrance and watched LP follow behind the guy as he drove away. He headed for his own car and headed for home. His day was done.

LP took up the pursuit. The man led him to the Troutman residence. He exited his pickup and went in the house. LP figured Mrs. Troutman would get an update tomorrow. There didn't appear to be much to report. He would get details from Phil in the morning. Hopefully the lady would want a couple of more days of this.

LP was right. There wasn't anything negative to report. Phil clocked in shortly after sunrise. LP offered to buy breakfast since he was financially liquid again. Over breakfast Phil reviewed the activity of the previous evening. "He certainly didn't look like a dedicated gambler. Who knows? Maybe he has to be in some certain mood to gamble. He didn't act like it yesterday."

"Did he appear to be discussing anything with anybody around him?"

"No. The guy looked like a lone wolf—a lost lone wolf."

"Well, when we get back to the office, I'll call her and give her the run down. She may just have to expect such behavior from a flaky amateur gambler. Just live with it. We'll see what she thinks."

Very shortly, LP called Mrs. Troutman at her work place. When LP suggested that her husband appeared to be a restless gambler, the lady vigorously disagreed. She said, "No. I know something more is going on. I don't want you to stop this investigation yet. Continue. I will come by at noon and give you more money if you wish."

LP replied, "OK. We will continue as you wish, and it would be fine if you want to stop by the office during the day and keep the books up to date. Someone will be here."

Later in the day, Phil stationed his car near the exit of the parking lot to take up chase after 5:00 p.m., if necessary. Today LP would follow Troutman when he finished the day's work.

Right on schedule, their man walked out of his work building. As he had on the previous day, he walked past the parking lot and proceeded to the gambling hall a block further up the street. He didn't show any signs that he suspected he was being followed.

LP waited briefly nearby before following him inside. He went to the lunch counter and ordered a Pepsi. There was a bowl of hard-boiled eggs near the cash register. He sat on a stool at the counter, peeled his egg, and enjoyed his drink while he watched his man through the back bar mirror on the wall. Troutman appeared to be giving a repeat performance of his actions of the day before. He sat at a table with four other players and didn't appear to be raking in any chips. He was just dribbling away his stack of chips.

After about twenty-five minutes, Troutman got up and headed for the door. LP followed and was led back to the parking lot. LP lingered outside nearby. He saw Phil parked nearby. He appeared to be reading a map or something. In a minute or so, Troutman drove out the gate in his crummy-looking pickup and headed up the street. LP's partner pulled out from the curb and entered traffic closely behind the pickup. It looked like Troutman was headed home like a good husband should. LP would see his partner in the morning for confirmation. He called it a day.

CHAPTER 28

s LP slipped the key into this office door, he thought, *Well, another day, another dollar. I hope, I hope.* At his desk he saw he had a phone message. He punched the replay button and heard the hysterical voice of Mrs. Troutman. In a quivering voice, she said, "Call me as soon as you get this message. It's terrible, it's terrible. It's horrible. I am at home, and the number is 336-4062."

LP dialed the number, and she answered after the first ring.

"This is Cinch. What seems to be the trouble? You sound quite upset."

She said, "The police came here last night and told me my husband had been killed. They said he was burned up in his car. He's dead. I thought you were following him all the time. How could something like this happen?" She sobbed into the phone.

LP waited a bit and said he was completely unaware this had occurred. "I don't know what to tell you."

She said the police officers had asked her a lot of questions. "I told them I had hired you to check on my husband and follow him. I gave them your name, and they said they would contact you early this morning. I'm so confused and frightened that I can't think. I'm going to stay home today, and I may go see a doctor or someone to help me through this. This can't be happening. If you find out why this happened, call me right away. Maybe they got my husband confused with someone else and he wasn't killed after all. He didn't come home last night, though, so maybe there is no hope."

LP said he would await the meeting with the police and call her back if he had any information.

LP thought for a minute about what he would do. It was after 8:00 a.m., and Phil hadn't arrived yet. He was usually at the door right at eight o'clock on the dot. LP could fill the cops in on his part of the pursuit last night. Mrs. T didn't have any info on anything, like where it happened or when it happened. She did say that her husband hadn't come home, though. That was interesting. If he didn't go home, then what the heck was Phil doing? LP doubted Troutman could give Phil the slip on the way home. LP decided he had to talk to Phil to fill in the cracks. The cops were also certainly going to go over this big time. LP called Phil's phone number. No answer. Now what?

LP decided to run over to Phil's apartment. It was just a short drive. Before he left the office, he left two messages on the door—one to Phil that said he was looking for him and one for the cops telling them he would be back in thirty minutes. This trip would take no longer.

Within minutes, LP parked his car in front of Phil's place. He lived in apartment twenty-two of a two-story apartment complex. The apartments surrounded a small courtyard and swimming pool, with a resident parking lot to the rear. After LP pounded on Phil's door several times with no response, Phil's neighbor came to his aid.

"Can I help you? I don't think he's home."

LP said, "I'm a pal of Phil's. Have you seen him around?"

"No. He sits around the pool a lot, but I didn't see him at the pool at all last night. You can hear your neighbor through these walls, and I haven't heard a sound from his place all morning."

"Do you know where he parks his car?" asked LP.

"All the tenants have their parking spaces in back. Phil lives in apartment twenty-two, so parking space number twenty-two would be where he'd park."

LP thanked the man and walked back to the parking lot. As expected, Phil's space was empty—no 1979 plain Ford Sedan with Oregon license plates. Phil had called it his perfect snooper car.

As he exited the creepy elevator in his office building, he saw two well-dressed gentlemen at his office door. He assumed this must be the expected visit from the fuzz.

He said, "Good morning, gentlemen. I understand you are looking for me. Let's go in to my spacious office." LP opened the door, and as they entered, the men showed LP their IDs. LP looked at one card and said, "Thank you, Detective Brown." He glanced at the other officer's card and said, "Thank you, Detective Green." He paused for a moment and then said, "You got to hand it to the county sheriff; the man does have a sense of humor." Neither officer showed any sign of amusement.

Detective Green said, "Tell us all you know about Mr. Troutman."

LP began with Mrs. Troutman's initial phone call. He concluded by saying, "The last time I saw Mr. Troutman was last night at about five thirty p.m. as he drove his pickup truck from the parking lot a block up the street. My partner, Phil Colt, followed a safe distance behind him. I assumed Troutman was headed home for the night. I have no idea what happened after that."

Detective Green said, "Well, where is Phil Colt? We need to get some details from him."

LP said, "That's the sixty-four-dollar question. I don't have a clue where he is this morning. I called his apartment early today and nobody answered, so I drove over to his apartment to see if he was there. A neighbor said he hadn't see Phil around the place last night or this morning. I also checked the parking lot up the street this morning to see if his car was over there. No car. That's where he usually parks during the day."

Detective Brown said, "Well, we've got to see him very shortly about this or his name is going on the wanted list."

Detective Green said, "Since you have actually seen Troutman a couple times, you could be of great help to us on one matter. Someone has to take a look at the corpse for identification purposes. We hate to make Mrs. Troutman go through that, so if you would agree to do that, it would be a big help for us."

"I'd be glad to," said LP, "and I even have a picture of the guy that I got from Mrs. T." LP pulled out the picture from his desk drawer and handed it to Green. "I'll tell the lady I turned it over to you in case she says she wants it back."

As they all drove to the morgue, LP said, "You know, I really don't know anything about the situation. Where in heck did this all happen?"

"It happened early last night about five miles out of town off the river road," said Green. "The fire occurred in a truck-loading area at the end of a dead-end road off the highway. At a little after seven p.m., a farmer nearby called the fire department to report a big fire and lots of smoke. When the firemen got there and saw they had a body in the burning car, they called the sheriff's department. The body was removed and taken to the morgue. There wasn't much left of the victim, and apparently the victim had been shot right in the face with a shotgun round. The victim had been sitting on his wallet, and there was some ID in it with Troutman's name on it. We also had the automobile license number to run down the name of the owner."

"There's not much left of the guy. Be prepared for what you are going to see this morning," said Brown.

"Was there any sign of my partner's car out there? It's an old Ford with Oregon plates on it."

"There were no cars at the scene," replied Green. "There was an old tractor and some machinery. That was it other than the burned pickup."

In the morgue, the body was rolled out for all to see. After LP viewed the body for several minutes, he said, "It's hard to say. The guy looks about the right height, but that's about all I can tell. I wouldn't say it's not him. Did you find anything in his pockets besides the wallet? Any car keys or anything?"

"No car keys; they were in the dash. We have a box of burned-up clothes, some coins, and that's about all. They're in a box in another room. Do you want to look at that stuff?"

"I might as well. I don't think it would hurt. I've got kind of a strange feeling about this deal. Let's take a look."

In the evidence box was a lot of totally burned clothing and one other item that triggered something in LP's mind. He remained silent for a long minute and then said, "What a cruel damned hoax. What a tragedy. I know who the killer is. The killer is Troutman. He's not the victim; he's the lousy killer. The guy in the other room is probably my partner, Phil Colt. If it's not, then it has to be someone who ripped off Phil's boots. These badly burned boots are the boots Phil wears every day. Yesterday when I trailed Troutman, I noticed he was wearing wing-tipped shoes, not boots. I definitely won't verify that the body we have here is Troutman. Why Troutman would kill Phil I don't know. There was no reason. I think before this week they were total strangers. My wild guess is that Mrs. Troutman is involved in this thing too. My guess is this is an attempted insurance scam and Troutman has a whole lot of life insurance policies floating around with his wife as the survivor. Otherwise I wouldn't have a clue on this. Why would he be blasted in the face with a gun, and why burn him to a crisp? Was the killer trying to kill the victim twice? I don't think so. He didn't want him identified correctly.

"My guess is Troutman left the scene of the crime in Phil's car, and I bet the car was left on the street somewhere near Troutman's home. Check the towing companies for an old Ford sedan with Oregon plates on it. There could be some evidence in it—who knows?"

The two cops said nothing. Both appeared to be in deep thought. LP couldn't tell if they bought his spiel or not.

LP continued, "You've got a big problem. Mrs. T could be involved, but can you prove that? The biggest issue is, can you find Mr. Troutman? He could be sitting somewhere up in the mountains trying to grow a big, bushy beard while he comes up with a new identity. Maybe he's counting that prospective pile of money he plans to get from the insurance people. When you find him and get him into court, those boots and my testimony should do the job. But if you can't run him down, I may consider going into the missing persons business. Damn! I'm going to miss old Phil Colt."

LP concluded, "Well, I guess I'm done here. I think I'll go back to the office. I don't need a ride. I can catch a crosstown bus right to my front door. Maybe by some miracle I'll find Phil sitting in my office with his bare feet propped up on my desk. What a miracle that would be."

There were no miracles in his office. LP began to think about the whole recent adventure. He wondered why the Troutmans had chosen LP and Phil to carry out their evil stunt. Likely they saw LP's ad in the paper, and when Mrs. Troutman checked into LP's miserable office, she was sold that LP was just the sap to swallow their plan. When he and Phil saw the cash, they followed like sheep, the perfect patsies.

And LP was one very lucky man. Had he chosen to follow Troutman by car on the second evening, he would have ended up dead in Troutman's car instead of Phil. LP said out loud, "Thanks, Phil, for taking my place and saving my life."

The crime was almost successful. If LP hadn't looked in that evidence box, they could have gotten off with murder for insurance money. They almost sold their plan, but they didn't. You might say they came close but no cigar.

CHAPTER 29

The next morning LP was viewed the world from the large office window and thought of the previous tragic morning. Suddenly he was struck by his plan to become a famous novelist. He wanted to write a great whodunit to satisfy the hunger of the literary world. Today was the day to start.

He removed a sheet of typing paper from a desk drawer and put it into his ancient mechanical Royal typewriter. His plan was to whip out five or six pages before someone could put him to work.

After several hours of deep thought and diligent typing, LP reviewed what he had shared with the world of potential readers. Already it had become a major undertaking, but he would conquer it. He read:

Chapter 1

It was Monday morning, eight o'clock and back to the grind. It was the start of another workweek, and LP Cinch was on his second cup of coffee, attempting to get his mind out of brain lock.

"Well, Cinch, did you do anything important over the weekend?" asked Irv Kluger, a fellow probation officer.

LP thought, *Boy, this is mentally demanding, and I am moving along at a snail's pace. Words of intrigue come only with great effort. I will need to pick up several items to get this book moving. I need one large dictionary and many bottles of Wite-Out. But no way will I be a defeatist. I can feel I am going to make a major breakthrough very shortly. Yes, this might take a little time and a lot of inspiration. And speaking of breakthroughs, this might be the time to slip out and pick up that dictionary and Wite-Out.*

CHAPTER 30

As LP stepped from the gloomy lobby of his building into the bright sunlight, he had the feeling that the old familiar saying "Close but no cigar" summarized life itself. We all spend our lives trying to drag our wagons up the mountain to its unreachable peak. No one really reaches the summit, but that is life. We just keep going because there is no other direction to take. And nobody actually knows what he or she wants or what to expect up there. We tread on because all of humankind is on the march. It's the only game in town.

One might as well stop now and then to rest and enjoy the view. You can trudge on later. LP decided the view was great today. He felt great, and he decided he didn't need a *cee-gar* today.

The End
(for now)

AUTHOR'S NOTES

At this point, I would like to thank all who braved through this saga of LP Cinch with me. As I embarked on this story, I knew very little about LP Cinch, but as the story progressed, I found him to be a likable, resourceful, and interesting fellow. Was he a bad person? He might say yes. I believe that from the minute he looked into Margareta's bulky handbag, he believed he might be committing a crime if he didn't walk down the road immediately and leave the money where it was. But he didn't. He realized that Earle and his two friends (and their dog) were incapable of arriving at any rational disposition for the money because they feared they could be accused of involvement in a homicide. Any instant wealth for them would have totally disrupted their lifestyle and most likely made them a target from all sides. LP encouraged the finders to report the find to the authorities, but they opposed it. LP reasoned the money in the hands of authorities would be like a drop of rain falling from the heavens to the sands of the Sahara Desert; now you see it and now you don't.

Consequently LP decided that all of this money—this little drop of rain—could be spent on projects that would help those who were affected by the murder and others who were deserving a better life. LP wouldn't monetarily profit from the venture. However, if he did his task properly, it could clean up a few of those marks on his soul that Thomas Merton said were there.

I want everyone to know that the entire LP Cinch adventure is total fiction. None of it is fact, and no harm was intended toward anyone, living or dead.

In closing, I would like to use the quotable, humorous salutations of two famous radio comedians, Bob and Ray. At the end of their radio program, they signed off with good, healthy humor. Bob would say, "Write if you get work," and Ray would conclude with, "And hang by your thumbs."

I'll write if I find work; otherwise you can look for me somewhere hanging by my thumbs.

Fait Accompli